DEATH OF A GLUTTON

DEATH OF A GLUTTON

M.C. Beaton

Chivers Press • G.K. Hall & Co.
Bath, Avon, England • Thorndike, Maine USA

This Large Print edition is published by Chivers Press, England, and by G.K. Hall & Co., USA.

Published in 1997 in the U.K. by arrangement with Transworld Publishers Ltd.

Published in 1996 in the U.S. by arrangement with St. Martin's Press, Inc.

U.K. Hardcover ISBN 0–7451–4940–5 (Chivers Large Print)
U.K. Softcover   ISBN 0–7451–4951–0 (Camden Large Print)
U.S. Softcover   ISBN 0–7838–1484–4 (Nightingale Collection Edition)

The text of this Large Print edition is unabridged.
Other aspects of the book may vary from the original edition.

Set in 16 pt. New Times Roman.

Printed in Great Britain on acid-free paper.

British Library Cataloguing in Publication Data available

Library of Congress Cataloging-in-Publication Data

Beaton, M. C.
    Death of a glutton / M. C. Beaton.
      p.   cm.
    ISBN 0–7838–1484–4 (lg. print : sc)
    1. Large type books.   2. MacBeth, Hamish (Fictitious character)—
Fiction.   3. Police—Scotland—Highlands—Fiction.   4. Scotland—
Fiction.   I. Title.
[PR6052.E196D39   1996]
823'.914—dc20)
                                                                            95–34483

TO JULIAN SPILSBURY

CHAPTER ONE

O fat white woman whom nobody loves
—FRANCES CROFTS CORNFORD

It was a blue day in the West Highlands of Scotland as P.C. Hamish Macbeth strolled along the waterfront of the village of Lochdubh. Not blue meaning sad, but blue coloured by a perfect day, blue coloured by the sky arching above and the sea loch below. Mountains rearing up were darker blue, marching off into a blue infinity of distance, as if Sutherland in the north of Scotland had no boundaries, but were some sort of infinite paradise of clean air and sunlight.

It had been a bad winter and a damp spring, but summer, which usually only lasts six weeks at the best of times in the far north, had finally arrived in all its glory, strange to the inhabitants who were used to rain and damp and high winds.

Little silken waves curled on the shore. Everything swam lazily in the clear light. Never had the roses in the little village gardens been more profuse or more glorious. Dougie, the gamekeeper on Colonel Halburton-Smythe's estate, told everyone who would listen that unusual blossoming meant a hard winter to come, but few wanted to believe him. It was as

1

if the whole of Lochdubh were frozen in a time capsule, with one perfect day following another. Life, never very energetic, slowed down to a crawl. Old quarrels and animosities were forgotten.

All this suited Hamish Macbeth's easygoing character. There had been no crime at all for some time; his superior and frequent pain in the neck, Detective Chief Inspector Blair of Strathbane, was on holiday somewhere in Spain. Hamish planned to walk along to the harbour for a chat with any fisherman who happened to be mending nets, and then perhaps he would go up to the Tommel Castle Hotel for a coffee with Priscilla Halburton-Smythe, once the love of his life if she only but knew it.

Fisherman Archie Maclean was sitting on the edge of the harbour wall, staring out at the loch where the boats rocked gently at anchor.

'Aye, it's a grand day, Hamish,' he said as the policeman came up.

'Not verra good for the fish,' rejoined Hamish amiably.

'The fish is chust fine. Fair jumping into the nets, Hamish. Got a cigarette on you?'

'You forget, I gave up a whiles back,' said Hamish regretfully. Would he ever get over that occasional longing for a cigarette? It would be great to light one up and puff away contentedly.

'Ah, well, I'll chust go along to Patel's and

2

get some.' Archie prized himself off the harbour wall. Both men walked in the direction of the village general store.

Priscilla Halburton-Smythe was just coming out of the store with a bag of groceries in her arms. 'I'll take these, Priscilla,' said Hamish. 'Where are you parked?'

'Round the side of the shop, Hamish. Morning, Archie.'

'Why are you doing the shopping?' asked Hamish curiously.

'Wanted an excuse to get away,' said Priscilla, unlocking the car.

Priscilla's father, Colonel Halburton-Smythe, had turned his home into an hotel after losing his money. The hotel was thriving. Mr Johnson, former manager of the Lochdubh Hotel, now closed, was running the business, and so Priscilla was usually carefree. But Hamish noticed she was looking rather strained.

'What's up?' he asked.

'Come back with me and we'll have something to drink and I'll tell you.'

Hamish got in the car. He glanced at her sideways, reflecting that she looked more beautiful than ever. Her golden hair shone with health and her skin was lightly tanned. She was wearing a sky-blue cotton dress with a broad white leather belt at the waist and her bare tanned legs ended in low-heeled brown leather sandals. Some of the old desire tugged at his

3

heart, but she was so cool and competent, so expert a driver, so seemingly oblivious of him as a man, that it quickly died. He felt illogically that she would be quite devastating if she did something wrong for once, crashed the gears, dropped something, had a hair out of place, wore the wrong shade of lipstick, or were guilty of any simple little human lapse at all.

The fake baronial pile that was Tommel Castle Hotel soon loomed up. She told Hamish to leave the groceries at the reception desk and then led the way through to the bar, formerly the morning-room. 'Want a whisky, Hamish, or will we have coffee?'

'Coffee's just fine.' She poured two mugs of coffee and they sat down at one of the tables.

'So what's been happening?' asked Hamish.

'Well, everything was running smoothly. The new gift shop that I am going to run is nearly finished and I've been off on my travels accumulating stuff to display in it. We were expecting eight members of a fishing club. But they cancelled at the last minute. Their chairman was trying to land a salmon somewhere down south and the fish turned out to be more powerful than he and dragged him in and down the rocks and over the rapids. He's recovering in hospital. He was an old friend of Daddy's and it turned out that Daddy hadn't even charged any booking-fees. So we had another booking which Daddy wanted to turn down flat. It's from the Checkmate

4

Singles Club. Daddy has gleaned a lot of knowledge of singles' bars from American films, and so the very word "singles" started him foaming at the mouth. Mr Johnson said, quite rightly, that we should take their booking to make up for the lost fishing party, but Daddy wouldn't be moved, so Mr Johnson called me in to talk sense into his head.

'This Checkmate Singles Club is actually one of the most expensive dating and marital agencies in Britain. I told Daddy they must have half the titles in the country on their books, which is a wild exaggeration, but the old snob fell for it,' remarked Priscilla, who often found her father a trial. 'It's actually mostly a marriage agency. The thing that clinched it was the woman who runs it, Maria Worth, dropped in on us to check the place out and she was so impeccably tweedy and blue-blooded—she even has a tweedy mind—that Daddy caved in and smarmed all over her. So everything's settled, but I felt so limp after all the arguments and stupidity, I felt I had to get away just for a little and volunteered to do the shopping.'

'You mean this Maria Worth is something like a marriage-broker?'

'Sort of. She charges enormous fees. She's bringing eight of her clients up to get acquainted.'

'Dear me,' said Hamish, scratching his fiery-red hair in puzzlement, 'they must be a sad

5

bunch of folk if they have to pay some woman to find them a mate.'

'Not necessarily. Usually they're people who want someone with money to match their own fortunes or middle-aged people who don't want to go through the indignities of dating a stranger. It's very hard dating in this day and age, Hamish,' said Priscilla seriously. 'I mean, isn't it better to have an agency check the other person out first? Find out all about them? I might try it myself.'

'Don't be silly,' said Hamish crossly. 'We both know almost everyone in the whole of damn' Sutherland and what we don't know we can soon find out.'

'Who says I want to marry someone from bloody Sutherland?' Priscilla glared at him.

Hamish suddenly grinned, his hazel eyes dancing. 'So you're human after all.'

'Of course I'm human, you great Highland drip.'

'It is just that you always seem so cool about everything, like a nice chilled salad.'

'I don't like scenes and confrontations, that's all. If you had a father like mine, you would shy away from dramatics as well.'

'Why doesn't the wee man just jack this hotel business in?' said Hamish, not for the first time. 'He's making a mint. He can go back to being lord of the manor and take down the hotel sign.'

'He loves it. Some of his old army friends

book in here and he tells them long stories about how he had nearly shot himself when he lost his money and how courageously he had fought back single-handed, just as if Mummy and I hadn't done all the work, not to mention Mr Johnson. It's the new legend. "The Plucky Colonel." Still, I'm being catty. He's happy. His rages don't mean anything. They never last for long, and then he can't even remember what all the fuss was about. Anyway, you're having a lovely life. No murders.'

'Thank goodness for that,' said Hamish. 'And not a cloud in the sky.'

*   *   *

But the clouds that were about to darken his tranquil sky in the shape of the members of the Checkmate Singles Club were soon approaching Sutherland.

On her road north a week later was the organizer, Maria Worth. She was a stocky, cheerful woman who had made a success out of the business. She never had large get-togethers for her clients. She always assembled them in small groups and in some romantic setting, but usually in or near London. She had heard from friends about the Tommel Castle Hotel and decided it would be a perfect setting for the most difficult of her clients. She would not have thought of such an adventurous scheme had Peta been around. Peta Gore was the bane

7

of Maria's otherwise successful life. Peta had put up half the money to launch Checkmate, becoming a partner. When the business flourished, Maria had tried to buy her out, but Peta refused. For Peta was a widow on the look-out for a husband and she hoped to pick up one at one of Maria's get-togethers. She never troubled her head with any of the nitty-gritty of office work or with interviewing or researching clients. But she had a nasty habit of turning up, uninvited, and throwing the carefully chosen guest-list out of sync.

Maria had come to hate her old friend. For not only was Peta noisy and vulgar, she was a glutton. There was no softer word for it. She was not just 'fond of her food' or had 'a good appetite,' she sucked and chomped and chewed with relish, all the while inhaling noisily through her nose. She was a party-pooper extraordinaire.

But Maria had been determined that Peta should not find out about the visit to Tommel Castle and so had kept quiet about it until Peta, thinking there was nothing in the offing, had said she was taking a holiday in Hungary.

Sitting in a first-class carriage on the Inverness train, Maria opened her Gucci brief-case and took out a sheaf of notes and thanked God that Peta was far away, slurping and chomping her way up and down the shores of the Danube.

She ran over her notes to double-check that

8

she had paired her singles correctly.

There was Sir Bernard Grant, who owned a chain of clothing stores. A photo of him was pinned to the notes. He was in his late forties, small, round, plump and clever. He was a widower. He had approached the agency because he had found himself too busy and too reluctant to begin dating again at his age. And by the time he joined, it was well known that Checkmate only catered to the rich.

Maria slid out the next sheet of paper. He was to be paired with Jessica Fitt, owner of a florist's shop in South Kensington. Jessica had a degree in economics from Newcastle University. After various jobs she did not like very much, she had taken a training in floristry, opened up a shop, and then used her excellent business brain to make it pay. She was a grey lady: grey hair, grey face, and she even wore grey clothes. In her shop, she had confided to Maria, she was deferred to by her staff and known by her regular customers. But outside the shop, people seemed to treat her as if she were invisible. She had recently come round to the idea that a husband would be a good thing, not for sex or romance, but to have someone with her who could catch the eye of the maître d' in a restaurant. Sir Bernard only wanted a wife because he needed a hostess. Yes, they should hit it off.

The next photograph showed a pleasant-looking young man with a square face, rather

9

small eyes, and a rather large mouth. This was Matthew Cowper, a yuppie, twenty-eight and surely the last person to need the aid of Checkmate. But he had climbed fast in the world from low beginnings and he wanted a wife with a good social background to help him go further. He expected Checkmate to introduce him to the sort of people he would not otherwise meet socially.

He was to be matched with Jenny Trask. Jenny was a legal secretary with a private income from a family trust. She was fairly attractive in a serious way: black hair and glasses, a good mouth, and large blue eyes. She was, however, painfully shy.

Maria put that lot to one side. The train roared across the border into Scotland. It had been muggy and overcast, but now the skies were clear blue and the sun was shining. And Peta was far, far away.

Maria smiled and returned to the rest of her notes. The good-looking features of Peter Trumpington smiled up at her from a large colour photograph. Now, *he* was a prize! He had a large fortune and did not work at anything at all, quite unusual in this age of the common man. But like any other rich man, he was tired of being preyed on and needed the agency to sort out the wheat from the chaff. He had been engaged to a film starlet who had relieved him of a sizeable chunk of money before dumping him. Then a typist caught his

10

eye, a typist whose looks hid the fact that she was dull and rather petty, but he had found that out in time and he had dumped *her*. Although tall and handsome, with dark hair and melting dark eyes, he did not have much personality. He also did not evince any signs of great intelligence.

So chosen for him was Deborah Freemantle, also with a private fortune, who worked as an editorial assistant to a publisher in Bedford Square, London. She still spoke like a schoolgirl with many exclamations of 'Gosh! I *say!*' and thought everything was FUN and had joined Checkmate for 'a giggle,' or so she said, although her parents had made the booking.

The last man on the list was John Taylor, Q.C.; in his sixties, widower, dry and chalky-skinned and fastidious, grey hair still quite thick, contact lenses, punctiliously dressed. He wished to be married again to spite his son and daughter. He hoped for someone young enough to still bear children but did not want 'some silly little bimbo.'

Selected for him was Mary French, a demure spinster in her early thirties. She was an English teacher at a public school, not *that* rich, but comfortably off and made up in breeding what she lacked in wealth, which had made her acceptable to Checkmate. She was third cousin to the Earl of Derwent. Maria squinted doubtfully down at the photograph. Mary was a teensy bit rabbit-toothed and

11

perhaps her ears did stick out a trifle, but then John Taylor was hardly an Adonis and he was quite old.

With an increased feeling of well-being, she packed away her notes and closed her eyes. Nothing could possibly go wrong.

* * *

Jessica Fitt, had Maria but known it, was further down the train in the second-class dining car, trying to catch the eye of the waiter so that she could order more tea, but the waiter slouched past her as if she did not exist. She gave a little sigh and wondered, as she had wondered so many times before, why she did not have the courage to raise her voice and call him. She thought of Checkmate and wondered whom they had found for her and experienced a sudden spasm of nerves that made her nervously scratch her armpits and then one hip. She belonged to that nervous breed of women who are forever scratching themselves. She did hope it would be different from the other two events organized by Checkmate: one dinner party, and one cocktail party in the Whistler Room at the Tate Gallery. The man selected as her escort on each occasion had drifted off to talk to some other woman. If it had not been for the attentions of Maria Worth, she would have been left entirely alone. But perhaps this time it would work. It was a

12

whole week in which to get someone to notice her. She sighed. Someone—anyone—kind would do. She had lost hopes of romance long ago.

* * *

Sir Bernard Grant drove his large car northwards through the clear empty Highland landscape. If he did not find a partner at this affair, he would drop Checkmate and try one of the other agencies. He was very rich, but that did not mean he liked wasting money, he told himself virtuously. He needed a wife, a good hostess, someone with a bit of style. He wasn't much interested in sex. He could always buy that.

* * *

Also driving north was Matthew Cowper, still young enough at twenty-eight to dream of a mixture of social success and romance. He wanted one of those cool society girls. For all there were a lot of yuppies like him working in brokerage houses in the City, chaps from ordinary working-class backgrounds, he knew the old guard stuck together. The correct wife would give him that edge he needed.

He turned in at the gates of the Tommel Castle Hotel, silhouetted against the blue sky, turrets and pinnacles and battlements and all.

13

It was a fake castle, built in Victorian times, but Matthew did not know that. It reminded him of a castle in a boy's book about knights of old that he used to treasure.

He saw Priscilla Halburton-Smythe walking across the drive in front of the castle and his heartbeat quickened. What a stunner! Thank you, God!

*   *   *

Jenny Trask had a lot in common with Jessica Fitt. Although she was attractive and in her twenties, she was painfully shy outside the confines of her job in a legal office. She hated dating because either the man dashed off right after dinner, which was a painful rejection, or he stayed on, obviously expecting the evening to end in bed. Jenny felt she did not belong to the world that her contemporaries inhabited. They thought nothing of leaping into bed with someone on a very short acquaintanceship. They were, or so Jenny thought, hard-headed and practical. Jenny dreamt of romance and longed for the days, now long gone, when a girl could expect to be courted. She had only recently joined Checkmate, and this visit to the Highlands was her first experience with the agency.

Hope sprang eternal. Jenny had flown to Inverness and then caught a bus to Ullapool, then changed at Ullapool to a creaking local

14

bus to take her to Lochdubh. Her hopes soared with every mile. So remote from London and so very beautiful. She was seeing the mountains and moors of Scotland as they are rarely seen, benign in sunlight. It had cost an awful lot of money, but already she felt sure it was all worth it. Somewhere at the end of the journey was the clever, sensitive, and romantic man of her dreams.

* * *

Peter Trumpington drove his Mercedes with the real leather seats competently through some of the most dazzling scenery in the world—like Switzerland without people—and was completely unaware of the beauty around him. He would have been just as happy in London. But if this long journey meant a suitable bride, then this long journey had to be completed. All that was in his mind was the thought of a long cool drink and a hot dinner. He did not know Deborah Freemantle had been chosen for him, or anything about her.

* * *

Deborah was also driving along the one-track roads near journey's end. She was employed as an editorial assistant with Dumbey's Publishing, who produced large coffee-table books on art or country houses or other

15

inoffensive and expensive subjects. She had been hired not for her brains, but because she did not expect to be paid very much, because her grammar was quite good and her enthusiasm boundless. She also had one great asset. She did not aspire to take her boss's job. Dumbey's was not a competitive firm, and editors liked to have inferiors who would not threaten their position. Her enthusiasm was not an act. She *was* genuinely enthusiastic about everyone and everything, which made up for her clumsiness and large backside. She had heavy Hanoverian features and rather thin brown hair. She bounced and giggled much as she had done at the expensive boarding-school she had once attended. She had made her come-out as a débutante, but things, her parents had decided, were not handled as in the old days, when a good dowry was enough to thrust a beloved daughter into marriage. Checkmate had been their idea. As with Jenny, this would be the first get-together she had attended. She was not very worried about it all. Mummy and Daddy usually knew best.

*   *   *

John Taylor, Q.C., alighted from the station at Inverness. He recognized Maria Worth, who was walking along the platform in front of him, but he did not hail her. To him, she was a sort of employee and he was not going to demean

16

himself by sharing his taxi north with her.

The taxi-driver he asked to take him to Lochdubh explained it would probably cost him in the region of forty-five pounds. 'Oh, get on with it,' snapped John, and climbed into the back seat.

Money was no object when it came to spiting his children. The trouble had started last Christmas in the family get-together at John Taylor's country home in Buckinghamshire. His wife had died when the children were still young, and he considered he had done the best anyone could for daughter Penelope and son Brian. Brian was a lawyer like his father and quite a successful one. Penelope had married an affluent stockbroker. All was what it should be.

And then, coming down the stairs one morning before Christmas, he had overheard Brian and Penelope talking.

'I wish we didn't have to endure these ghoulish family affairs,' Brian was saying. 'The old man has about as much Christmas spirit as Scrooge.'

Penelope gave her infuriating giggle and said, 'He hasn't been quite the same since they abolished hanging. He's still boring on about bringing back the birch and the treadmill.'

And Brian had rejoined, 'Only a few more days to go and then we can escape from his pontificating. But be sweet to him, Penelope. Your kids and my kids will soon be ready to go

17

to public schools and you know what a mint that's going to cost us. He can't last much longer. He looks like cadaver warmed up. He's made his will and we both get the lot. So let's continue to ho-ho-ho our way through this awful Christmas.'

John had retreated back upstairs. Hatred burned inside him. To cut them out of his will would not be revenge enough. After he was dead, he wouldn't be around to see their stupid faces. He thought long and hard about ways to get even and then he decided to go to Checkmate and order them to find him a bride. They probably had someone on their books desperate enough.

*   *   *

Mary French had already arrived at Tommel Castle Hotel. Mary was always early for everything. She turned up at dinner parties at least an hour early. She had taken the train up to Inverness the day before and had got the first bus in the morning to Ullapool and then a cab from Ullapool to Lochdubh. She was not nervous in the slightest. Maria Worth might regret the fact that Mary had buck-teeth and jug-ears, but Mary saw rare beauty when she looked in the glass. She taught at a girls' school, one of the few that still employed only female teachers. That was why, she knew, she was not married. Men could only admire her from afar. The fact that she met plenty of men on her annual holidays did not count. Her aristocratic breeding had put them off. Checkmate would find her the right sort. They'd better, she thought with true aristocratic thrift. She was paying enough.

* * *

Maria got down to business with Mr Johnson as soon as she arrived. There was to be a drinks party before dinner; not in the bar, but in a small private room off the dining-room.

Priscilla Halburton-Smythe was upstairs in her room, cursing as she took out a black dress. Two of the waitresses had gone off sick with summer colds. She could not risk getting some untrained woman from the village. She would need to act as waitress herself, and that meant taking round the trays of drinks before dinner as well. Thank goodness her father retained enough distaste for Checkmate not to want to play 'mine host,' or he would foam and huff and puff at the sight of his daughter in a waitress's uniform, blissfully unconcerned that if she did not help, the dinner would be a disaster.

The programme for the week had been posted up in each of the Checkmate clients' bedrooms. They were expected to present themselves for drinks at six-thirty. Priscilla went along the corridor to the maid's cupboard and selected and tied on an apron. She

19

hesitated over the cap but then decided she had better put one on and look the part.

She went down to the bar at six-thirty. Jenkins, the Halburton-Smythe's former butler, now the maître d'hôtel, gave her a scandalized look as she walked through the hall. Jessie, the one waitress on duty, followed Priscilla into the room off the dining-room. Maria was already there, wearing a scarlet evening gown. The barman was ready to take orders. All Priscilla and Jessie had to do was go to the bar and fetch them and, after that, serve the dinner, which Jenkins, with averted eyes, told her was all ready.

Maria saw nothing wrong with the daughter of the house acting as waitress. Tommel Castle was a terribly expensive hotel and she expected the best of service.

'I have checked the place-settings,' said Maria. 'Everything is correct. The right people will be sitting next to each other. Nothing can go wrong. They should be here any minute.'

And then she looked over Priscilla's shoulder to the doorway and turned a muddy colour. Startled, Priscilla turned round.

A large fat woman was standing there. Her hair was dyed a flaming red. She was wearing a huge loose flowered blouse over a pair of trousers and an old-fashioned corset, to judge from the bumps and ridges. Her small, cornflower-blue eyes were sunk in pads of fat, and she had a small, petulant mouth.

20

'Surprise!' she cried.

Maria recovered with an effort. 'Peta,' she said in a hollow voice. 'What are you doing here? I thought you were in Hungary.'

'Changed my mind,' said Peta triumphantly. 'I called in at your office this morning and that silly secretary of yours said she didn't know where you were. So I checked the computer and found the address. I got the plane to Inverness and a cab up. Don't you think I'm clever?'

Maria rallied with a visible effort. 'Peta, I'm sure this isn't your scene.'

'Darling, of course it is. You know me . . . the merry widow. Oh, there she is. You haven't met my niece, Crystal Debenham, have you? Just back from finishing school in Switzerland.'

Maria stared. Disaster upon disaster. Crystal was so very beautiful in a smouldering kind of way: voluptuous figure, smoky-blue eyes, masses of brown hair highlighted with silvery-blonde streaks, pouting mouth, and wearing a dress so short it made her long, long legs look like a dream of desire. What man was going to look at any of her female clients with Crystal around?

'Pleased to meet you,' said Crystal in a languid, husky voice. She would have once, thought Priscilla, half-amused, half-exasperated, been called a vamp.

'Perhaps there are no rooms free, Peta *dear*,'

21

said Maria.

'No, I called before I left London and got a couple of rooms.'

'Wouldn't you like to change?'

'I never go in for that formal stuff,' said Peta cheerfully. She turned round. 'This your lot?'

Headed by Mary French, who would have been there much earlier had she not laddered two pairs of tights and spent some time looking for another pair, came the clients of Checkmate.

Crystal just stood and smouldered. The men clustered round her and the females stood a little way away, watching gloomily, not even talking to each other.

'What can I get you to drink?' Priscilla asked Maria.

'Get me a double gin,' said Maria waspishly. She looked at Peta with loathing.

'And get a double arsenic for her.'

CHAPTER TWO

The best laid schemes o' mice and men,
Gang aft a-gley

—ROBERT BURNS

To Maria's relief, the little knot of men around Crystal began to break up and she was able to seize arms and introduce the various clients to their proper partners. Crystal pouted slightly and swayed over to join her aunt.

The fact was, thought the ambitious Matthew Cowper shrewdly, that Crystal Debenham was the kind of girl one took to the pub to impress the other fellows. She was not the kind one married. She was extremely dull and had no talent for conversation whatsoever, the narcissistic Crystal considering looks enough.

Maria made it firmly obvious who was meant for whom, and Matthew was not sure that Jenny Trask was at all suitable. She was painfully shy and he wanted a firm, confident woman to help him in his career. The blonde beauty he had seen on his arrival, the one he had been so sure was meant for him, had turned out to be nothing more than an hotel waitress. He glanced at Priscilla and now saw only the uniform and not the beauty.

Jenny, ever polite, was struggling to make

23

conversation by telling him about her job. He barely listened, his eyes roving over the rest of the females and coming to rest on Mary French, the schoolteacher, she of the sticking-out ears and buck-teeth. Now *there* was class, from her pale, arrogant, self-satisfied look to her pearls and expensively dowdy dress. She had a hectoring carrying voice. He waited until Jenny had paused for breath, said, 'Excuse me,' and slid off.

John Taylor was relieved to see him. Although he was well aware that he, John, was old and could not expect a young beauty to be put his way, Mary appalled him. When Matthew came up, John crossed the room and joined Jenny, found out she was a legal secretary in Lincoln's Inn Fields in an office near his own, and happily began to talk shop.

Sir Bernard Grant barely saw the grey Jessica Fitt. He could not believe this was to be his partner. So he looked beyond Jessica's dull face, looking for another candidate, and fell on Deborah Freemantle, who was bouncing and wriggling in front of Peter Trumpington. He heard her loud laugh and decided she looked like more fun than anyone else there. So he joined her, and Peter Trumpington, who for all his shallow-mindedness was nonetheless kind, went to speak to Jessica Fitt.

Maria took a deep breath of relief. They were not pairing off the way she had intended, but at least they were all talking to each other

24

and the beautiful Crystal was ignored. Besides, once they found their place cards at the dinner table, they would once more be with their rightful partners.

But when she led the way into the dining-room, it was to find that Peta had already taken the chair at the head of the table, with Crystal next to her. Then the others just ignored the place cards and sat down and talked to the person they had been talking to before.

The first course was cock-a-leekie soup, Tommel Castle priding itself on its traditional Scottish dishes. Peta rolled up her sleeves and got to work. She gurgled, she slurped, she *inhaled* soup like a human vacuum cleaner, first breaking great clumps of bread into it and mashing them up with her spoon.

'Who on earth is that great fat woman?' muttered Sir Bernard to Deborah. Deborah laughed wildly and said, 'Gosh! I don't know. Sickening, isn't she?' and Sir Bernard began to think more and more that Deborah was his kind of girl.

The soup was followed by dishes of prawns in a delicate sauce. Peta wolfed hers down and turned to John Taylor, who was on her other side and looking at her in horrified amazement, said, 'I see you're not eating yours,' and before he could protest, snatched his dish and ate those too.

The next course was unfortunately a rich venison casserole with a wine sauce and the

25

casserole was placed at the head of the table in front of Peta. Peta waved Priscilla away and said she would serve. So the others soon found themselves looking down at small portions and then at the heaped mound of meat and sauce on Peta's plate. She bent down and snuffled at it appreciatively before diving in. She also ate great piles of vegetables and three large baked potatoes with a whole dairy of butter. She then called for more bread and, pulling the casserole close to her ballooning bosom, she began to mop up the gravy, making appreciative smacking sounds with her lips.

Priscilla was sorry for Maria. She wanted to tell her that her party was going to be a success, not despite Peta, but because of Peta. They were all being drawn together by a communal resentment. And Crystal, because of being the horror's niece, had rapidly lost any charms she might have had in the eyes of the assembled men.

The dessert was unfortunately meringues with cream and chocolate sauce. Powdered meringue soon dusted the glutton's face, almost covering up the gravy stains. When the petits fours came along, Peta upended the plate of them into her capacious handbag. 'I'll keep these for later,' she said, beaming all around.

Maria turned to the hovering Priscilla and said in a thin voice, 'Coffee in the lounge, I think, and some more petits fours, please. Peta, darling, you have had an exhausting journey.

26

Why don't you go and lie down?'

'You know, I think I might,' said Peta and yawned, a cavernous yawn, showing a coated tongue and bad teeth. She winked at Sir Bernard, 'I'll see you in the morning, sweetie.'

Crystal floated off in the wake of her aunt. Maria arranged her guests in a corner of the lounge, glad no other hotel guests were present.

John Taylor rose to his feet and hooked his thumbs into his waistcoat and faced the group with that steely look in his eye and commanding appearance which had made him a highly paid prosecuting counsel. He began his cross-examination. 'Now, Miss Worth, tell us ("in your own words," thought Jenny) about this Peta woman. Who is she?' He stabbed a finger at Maria. 'Why is she here? Is she one of your clients? Tell us.'

'If you will allow me to speak, I will,' said Maria, who had already made up her mind what she had to do. 'Mrs Peta Gore is my partner. She put up half the money to help me get started. I tried to buy her out last year, but she would not go. I tried to keep this excursion to the Scottish Highlands a secret from her and I thought she was in Hungary. But she found out where I was. This has happened before, but not at anything so ambitious as this. So I am going to make you an offer. Each of you. Anyone here who has not found a marriage partner by the end of the week will have the

27

cost of the hotel bill and travel refunded.'

There was a long silence. Then Deborah spoke up. 'I think that's jolly fair,' she cried. Sir Bernard said, 'I'll accept that,' and the others nodded agreement. John sat down feeling rather sulky. He had expected Maria to excuse and protest like a criminal in the dock. But she had behaved handsomely and spoilt his fun.

Priscilla bent over the table and arranged the coffee-pots. John said suddenly, 'You know, my memory's going. I feel I've seen someone in this group before, but in court.'

There were startled gasps. 'Who?' cried Deborah, bouncing up and down on her large bottom. 'You mean we might have a chain-saw murderer amongst us?'

John shook his head. 'I'm probably wrong. The trouble is, I see so many criminals that everyone begins to look like one.'

Jenny Trask said, 'I remember that famous case where you were the prosecutor for the Crown, that triple murderer, Jackson.'

'Tell us about it,' suggested Maria, accepting a cup of coffee from Priscilla.

He began to talk. Priscilla, standing on duty in the corner with the other waitress, remembered reading about the case in the newspapers. She felt uneasy. There never had been, surely, any really concrete evidence, and yet John Taylor had done a brilliant job and the man had gone to prison for life. Even talking about the case, John ceased to be a

28

tired-looking man in his sixties and became enlivened with fire and venom. A columnist had once written that his success was due to the fact that he appeared to have a genuine hatred of the people he was prosecuting. The legal department of the newspaper must have had too liquid a lunch that day, for the column was printed and John Taylor had sued the newspaper for some reportedly vast sum, although the whole thing was settled out of court. And the female columnist came out of it unscathed because she was having an affair with the newspaper proprietor.

Then Priscilla saw her father coming into the room. The colonel had learned that there was an eminent Queen's Counsel among the guests and so had decided to favour them with his presence. When the barrister had finished speaking, he asked them grandly if they were comfortable and then his choleric eye fell on his daughter in cap and apron.

'What the hell do you think you're doing dressed up as a waitress?' he roared.

'Sheena and Heather are off sick,' said Priscilla calmly. 'I had to help out.'

'Consult me next time you think of slumming,' raged the colonel. 'My own daughter!'

Mr Johnson, the manager, used to averting scenes, came quickly into the room and muttered something in the colonel's ear and drew him out.

29

Matthew Cowper had just learned from Mary French that she was the Earl of Derwent's third cousin, but the news that the blonde beauty was the daughter of the house made him look at Priscilla speculatively and he hardly heard what Mary was saying. He glanced round the lounge, formerly the drawing-room, of the well-appointed hotel. Must be a mint of money here, not that it was money he was after, but it all helped. This Priscilla was a stunner, and classy, too. She did not have the vulgar sultry beauty of Crystal, and any girl who mucked in and acted as a waitress wouldn't be too snobby.

Maria was just announcing that she had arranged a trip out on a fishing boat the following morning, urging them to be ready early, for Peta slept late. Matthew wondered whether to skip that trip and try his luck with the fair Priscilla.

But when they all finally rose to go to bed, he volunteered to help Priscilla clear away the coffee-things. She gave him a cool smile and said firmly, 'That won't be necessary.'

He thought that after all she might be a sheer waste of time and went upstairs to set his alarm.

Jenny Trask lay awake a long time. No knight on a white charger had come along. She was bitterly disappointed in Checkmate. Matthew Cowper was the sort of young man she would normally have gone out of her way to avoid, that was, if such a young man had ever shown an interest in her. Nothing was as she had expected it to be. And that dreadful Peta! Someone should put that woman out of everyone else's misery.

*   *   *

Hamish Macbeth was roused from gentle dreams about nothing very much by a hammering at the door. He crawled out of bed and went to answer it. 'Why, Archie,' he said, recognizing the fisherman, 'what's wrong?'

'Naething's wrong,' said Archie with a grin. 'I forgot to tell you that I'm taking a party frae the castle out on the boat the day and I wunnered if you would like to come along and gie me a bit o' a hand. Grand day and free food.'

Hamish thought quickly. Blair was away in Spain. Nothing had happened recently. 'Is herself coming?' he asked hopefully.

'Aye, I think I heard Miss Halburton-Smythe wass coming along,' lied Archie.

'Yes, I'll join you. What time?'

'Eight o'clock. They are haffing their breakfast on the boat.'

Hamish said goodbye to him and began to wash and dress quickly. He checked his sheep had water and fed his hens, and then ambled along the waterfront in the direction of the harbour. The day was as perfect as all the

31

previous days.

Jessie and Nessie Currie were standing by their garden gate. Hamish tried to walk past quickly, but Jessie said severely, 'And where are you going, young man? Where are you going?'

'Just along to the harbour,' said Hamish evasively.

'I noticed you haven't your uniform on, you haven't your uniform on,' remarked Jessie, who had an irritating habit of saying things twice over.

'Undercover work,' said Hamish desperately. 'Drug smugglers.'

'My, my!' marvelled Nessie. 'They get everywhere, don't they. It was saying on the telly...'

But Hamish had moved on. He felt it was odd to be walking through this Mediterranean landscape. No clouds marred the sky. A normal Scottish Highland day would either be weeping misty drizzle, or high winds with cloud shadows chasing each other down the flanks of the mountains and fitful gleams of sunlight. Archie's fishing boat, the *Jaunty Lass*, lay still at anchor.

Hamish climbed on board. 'I thought ye would have found more help, Archie,' he said. 'Where's your crew?'

'Say to a man they willnae stir frae their beds for a lot of rich English parasols.'

'Parasites?' suggested Hamish.

32

'Aye, them. Anyways, all you've got to do is help me cast off and then take a wee turn at the wheel. Sean Gallagher, the cook frae the castle, is cooking the breakfast in the galley. All we really have tae do is sharpen up the old knife and fork and dig in wi' the rest o' them.'

*   *   *

'What?' Priscilla stared sleepily at the hotel manager, who had come to rouse her. 'What do you mean, Sean is refusing to go?'

'Just that, the wee scunner,' said Mr Johnson with feeling. 'He says he gets seasick. He says nobody told him he had to cook on a boat. He says it's beneath him.'

'What's he gone temperamental for?' said Priscilla crossly. 'He's from Glasgow, not Paris. Did you threaten to fire him?'

'I wouldnae dare. He might go, and then where would we get another cook to match him? So I thought ... you see, it's not really cooking. Jist a kedgeree for breakfast and a cold lunch, and the lunch is all packed up.'

Priscilla groaned. 'Meaning you want me to go?'

'Well, it's a grand day out for ye.'

'All right. All right. But I know why Sean isn't going, and it's nothing to do with seasickness. He was raving on about that glutton, Peta, last night. Said she was an insult to his art. The idiot came up to the doorway of

33

the dining-room during the serving of the main course and he saw that big woman guzzling most of it. He went off and got drunk. I'll handle it, but don't tell Daddy.'

* * *

Ian Chisholm, the local garage owner, had renovated an old Volkswagen minibus, after he had learned that a party at the castle would be needing transport. He had sprayed the front of it bright red and then run out of that particular colour of paint, and so he had sprayed the rest primrose yellow. It had an odd carnival appearance, but at least the new coat of paint hid all the rust. The seats were badly damaged, as the previous owner had used it as a hen coop, but his wife had made some nice chintz loose covers to hide the defects.

Jenny, first to climb on board, felt her spirits lift. The ridiculous bus, combined with another beautiful day, made her feel she was indeed on foreign territory, with the pollution and bustle of London so far away. Matthew Cowper was next. He saw her, backed off the bus, waited until Mary French had taken a seat, and then got back on and sat down next to her. 'Social-climbing little runt,' thought Jenny bitterly and then reminded herself that she did not want him anyway, and as she was bound to be partnerless at the end of the week, she would get a refund, and so she should make the best of

34

this free holiday. The next to arrive was John Taylor in an old blazer, white panama hat, and white trousers, looking as if he were going to Henley Regatta rather than to a West Highland fishing boat. He raised his hat to Jenny and then sat down next to her. Outside the bus stood Maria Worth holding a clipboard which she felt made her look efficient. She was praying they would all get off before Peta rose and decided to join them. She did not relax until they were all on the bus, Deborah shrieking with delight at the chintz seat covers.

Jenny noticed Priscilla had joined the party, after overseeing the packing of cartons into the back of the bus.

The engine rattled and coughed and then finally roared into life. Off they went down the drive and out onto the one-track road which led down into the village of Lochdubh. Purple heather was blazing in all its glory, and far above two buzzards sailed lazily in the clear sky.

Priscilla stood up and faced the passengers. She was wearing a white blouse and a short denim skirt. She balanced easily in the swaying bus and her clear voice rose above the noise of the engine. 'I have brought along some bottles of sun-barrier cream,' she said. 'The air up here is very clear and you can get very badly burned indeed unless you take the necessary precautions.'

35

I would like to be like that, thought Jenny. Cool and competent.

Lochdubh was calm and quiet under its Sunday torpor: rows of little white cottages, a few shops, and then the harbour.

A tall, red-haired man with hazel eyes and an engagingly shy smile welcomed them on board the *Jaunty Lass*. He was wearing a faded blue shirt and faded blue jeans. Jenny smiled shyly back at him, her interest quickened. Here was the sort of man she could go for. Not some pushy lout of a yuppie like Matthew Cowper. She wondered what it would be like to be a fisherman's wife in this remote spot. Her romantic soul visualized living in one of those little cottages, waiting at dawn with a ragged tartan shawl about her shoulders and her hair streaming in the wind for the fishing boats to come home.

Then the dream was rudely shattered as she heard Priscilla hail the red-haired man with, 'Hullo, copper. Why aren't you on your beat, Hamish?'

'Archie asked me to help out,' rejoined Hamish. 'And what is yourself doing here?' he added, not wanting her to know that the reason for his own presence was because Archie had told him she would be with the party.

'Sean Gallagher's got the sulks, so I've to do the cooking, Hamish. So you can start by helping me load these boxes.'

'Can I help?' asked Jenny eagerly.

Priscilla smiled. 'You're on holiday. Go and find a nice seat in the sun.'

Jenny watched as Hamish and Priscilla, with the help of the driver and Archie Maclean, carried the boxes on board. She noticed that Hamish and Priscilla had the ease and familiarity of old friends. But they were not engaged. Priscilla wore no ring. There was hope yet.

'Is that everything?' asked Maria.

'Yes, all set,' said Hamish. 'I'll just cast off. Wait a bit. Are you expecting anyone else? That's the castle Range Rover coming down the hill at a fair pace.'

'No,' screamed Maria in sudden panic. 'Get going, man, for God's sake.'

Hamish quickly loosened the ropes from the capstans, shouted to Archie they were all set, and sprang on board. The short gangplank had already been pulled up. But Archie was fumbling about in the wheel-house as the Range Rover roared nearer, the horn going and the lights flashing. It screeched to a halt on the harbour and Peta lumbered down.

'Wait!' she called.

'Can't!' shouted Maria cheerfully. 'Too late!'

But Archie had nipped down from the wheel-house and was looking at her in surprise. He was hoping for tips, and as far as he was concerned, the more the merrier. 'Och, it won't

37

take a minute to get her on board,' he said. 'Hamish, jump down and tie her up again.'

The passengers watched gloomily as Hamish sprang onto the harbour. As he busied himself with the ropes he said to Mr Johnson, who had brought Peta, 'Couldn't you have driven a bit slower? Nobody seems to want her.'

'Are you kidding?' demanded the manager. 'She was screaming at me the whole way. If she'd had a whip, she'd have lashed at me to make me go faster.'

The gangplank was lowered. Peta waddled on board wearing a huge loose flowered dress like a tent. 'Gosh, I'm starving,' she cried. 'When's breakfast?'

'Any minute now,' said Priscilla. 'Archie, Hamish will need to help me in the galley.'

'What's for breakfast?' asked Hamish. 'Bacon and eggs?'

'No, kedgeree. I've a big pot of it. Sean keeps a ton of the stuff in the freezer and I defrosted it before I left. Heat up the rolls, Hamish, and put out the butter. Give them all a plate, cup, knife and fork—you'll find them in that box over there—and then the coffee and tea's in those giant flasks. They're the kind with spouts, so all you've got to do is twist and pour. Serve Peta first and that'll keep her quiet.'

Jenny came down into the galley. 'I'm sure you need help,' she said, but she looked at Hamish and not Priscilla.

To Priscilla's annoyance, Hamish promptly

38

relayed the orders she had just given him to Jenny. 'Now what are you going to do?' asked Priscilla, half exasperated, half amused as Jenny bustled off.

'I'll light the stove for you. It's tricky,' said Hamish, 'and then when you've got the kedgeree heated, I'll hold the casserole while you dish it out.'

'I hope you won't faint from exhaustion before the day is over,' said Priscilla sarcastically.

'I'll do just fine.'

When the kedgeree was heated, Priscilla piled a plate high and handed it to Jenny, who was now waiting behind her. 'Take that to Peta,' said Priscilla. 'There's loads here. Tell her to leave room for lunch.'

The members of Checkmate were sitting on the small deck. Peta broke off flirting with Sir Bernard when she saw the food arrive. Her eyes gleamed. Jenny cast one horrified look at Peta shovelling kedgeree into her mouth and darted off down the companion-way to get the food for the others. She felt brisk and efficient and quite confident now that she had something to do. She hoped that attractive policeman noticed just how brisk and efficient she was.

A policeman's wife might be no bad thing. He was, she judged, in his thirties and should surely have been promoted to a higher rank by now if he were any good. But with a wife behind him, he might do wonders. He looked

39

clever. She could see him now, solving cases in a sort of Lord Peter Wimsey way, throwing in the occasional apt quotation.

But that dream dissolved when she got downstairs again. Hamish was lying on one of the bunks, reading a newspaper. He did not look the least like an ambitious man.

Feeling slightly flat, she served the others before taking her own plate and sitting down to join them. The kedgeree was excellent, but they were all picking at their food and it was obvious they were trying to look anywhere and everywhere but at the glutton. Priscilla had made the mistake of bringing the remains of the casserole up, which Peta seized with both hands. She not only ate that but cleared up everyone else's leftovers. She was a mess of crumbs and rice and fish. This mess, once temporarily sated, began to flirt again with Sir Bernard, who edged away from her and asked Deborah if she would like to go to the side and see if there were any seals.

'Probably basking on rocks in this weather,' said Deborah, but she joined him at the side. And then Sir Bernard felt a pudgy arm steal about his neck and Peta's cooing voice saying, 'You know, you're my sort of man.'

Her fishy breath fanned his cheek. He could feel her blubbery body pressed against his side and wondered desperately why it was that men were always being accused of sexual harassment and never women. He had never before felt at such a loss, he, the business tycoon, who was used to handling all sorts of situations. He remembered visiting one of his stores to talk to the manager. He was leaving by walking through the shop after closing time when he had seen a light on in one of the fitting rooms. He had pulled back the curtain to switch the light off and had been confronted by a shop girl clad only in bra and pants, who had wet her lips and smiled at him seductively and he had immediately known she had staged the whole thing, had known he would leave by the shop floor and would see the light. He had jerked the curtain closed and had gone to fetch the manger, knowing the girl would be dressed by the time he returned. He therefore did not mention how he had found her but demanded the manager interrogate her as to why she was still on the premises after closing time. She made some lame excuse about getting ready to go to a party. He had drawn the manager aside afterwards and told him to wait three months, then find fault with the girl and sack her, and in the intervening period, he never went near the store. He had handled that properly. But there was something so repulsive, so frightening about Peta. She caused emotional claustrophobia. There was something almost cannibalistic about her. He jerked away from her and said desperately, 'Now, now, Mrs Gore, you will be making my fiancée jealous.'

Peta looked at him sulkily. 'Fiancée? What

fiancée?'

'Deborah,' said Sir Bernard.

'Oh, well . . .' Peta rolled off in the direction of John Taylor to try her luck there.

'Sorry about that,' said Sir Bernard awkwardly. 'I shouldn't have said that. You must be very embarrassed.'

'Gosh, no,' said Deborah. 'I was awf'ly flattered. For a moment I thought you meant it. Never mind. Look at that rock over there. What an odd shape.'

Sir Bernard looked at her fondly. She was far from pretty with her heavy face and limp brown hair, not to mention the backside, which was shown in all its glory in a brief pair of striped shorts, but she was clean and healthy and a good sort. Nothing messy or clingy about her.

'I don't know that I didn't mean it,' he said, taking her hand. 'But it doesn't do to rush things.'

'Gosh, no,' said Deborah. 'I mean, we hardly know each other. I feel like one of those Victorian heroines. "This is so sudden." Chin up! I'm not going to sue you for breach of promise.' But she left her hand in his and the pair suddenly beamed at each other.

Thank God, thought Maria, covertly watching them. 'Not what I had intended, but who cares? Oh, if only Peta would fall overboard.'

The headland fell away and the boat

42

chugged on into the oily swell of the Atlantic. Down in the galley, Priscilla said to Hamish, 'Get up and help me start preparing the lunch. I'm beginning to feel seasick.'

Hamish amiably swung his long legs down from the bunk. 'Show me where the stuff is and then take yourself up on deck for a breath of fresh air.'

'It's cold salmon for lunch. The hollandaise is in that plastic container and the other container holds the salad-dressing. You've got to tear up the lettuce and stuff in that box and make a big bowl of salad. Then there's quails' eggs to be shelled and salted. Lots of French bread. The wine's still cold and it's in that crate over there, along with some beer in case anyone wants that. Oh, Jenny, what is it?'

'The skipper's complaining that he wants some real food. He couldn't eat the kedgeree. He says it's foreign muck.'

'He's got some bacon and eggs here,' said Hamish, stooping down and looking in a small cupboard. 'Fry him up some and add a couple of slices of fried bread and then give him a cup of strong black tea and he'll be happy. You *are* looking a bit green, Priscilla. Off with you. We'll manage.'

Priscilla took in great gulps of fresh air and then went into the wheel-house. 'Can you find us somewhere on dry land for lunch, Archie?' she yelled above the noise of the engine.

'There's Seal Bay if I turn down the coast,'

43

said Archie, swinging the wheel. 'Usually too rough to get near it, but it should be chust fine the day.'

Priscilla went back out and joined Maria. 'How's it going?' she asked.

'No one seems interested in the ones I chose for them,' mourned Maria. 'I must be losing my touch. And Peta! What a disaster. Look, she's oiling around John Taylor and he's walked away from her several times.'

'The others seem all right,' said Priscilla. Sir Bernard and Deborah were holding hands, Peter Trumpington was being charming to Jessica Fitt—Jessica, who had actually managed to find a grey ensemble even for holiday wear; grey blouse with a thin white stripe and grey trousers. Matthew Cowper was showing off to MaryFrench, who was looking as smug as any woman who thinks she is a combination of Cleopatra and Princess Di usually looks.

And then Peta abandoned John and lumbered towards Matthew Cowper. 'Oh, dear,' said Maria. 'Now would you look at her! She thinks she's irresistible to men, no matter what age. I sometimes think all that food has lodged somewhere in Peta's brain. She's barmy.'

Matthew was backing towards the side of the boat away from Peta, who was flirting and ogling. And then Priscilla saw the sudden naked hatred in Mary French's eyes as she

44

looked at Peta and shivered despite the heat.

'You must send her away,' said Priscilla urgently.

'Peta? My dear girl, I would if I could. We'll all just need to survive the week.'

'But she's repulsive. There's something awful about her,' said Priscilla. 'She's the sort of woman who gets killed.'

'No hope of that,' said Maria.

The boat had swung in towards the shore, bucking up and down in the landswell.

Soon Priscilla recognized the sandy cove which was Seal Bay. It was a beautiful spot, almost inaccessible from the land and barely accessible from the sea except on rare summer days like this.

The *Jaunty Lass* chugged into calm water and then the engines died. Hamish appeared from below and helped Archie to drop anchor and then they lowered the boat's dinghy, Hamish going first to row the lunch ashore. He had had to do very little preparation. Jenny had fixed everything, even Archie's breakfast, and Archie, feeling he had had 'proper' food, was joining in the holiday atmosphere.

Peta demanded to go ashore before the rest. By common consent, she was allowed the dinghy to herself. Hamish, rowing her ashore, hoped she would not sink the dinghy, for she was so heavy that the stern was dangerously low in the water.

She climbed out, wading through the

45

shallows, and then flopping on the sand like a beached whale.

Soon they were all on shore and Jenny was spreading a white table-cloth on the sand. Peta sat at the edge of the cloth with a fork in one hand and a knife in the other, her piggy eyes gleaming. Priscilla was glad of Jenny's efficient help, although she knew Jenny was doing it all for Hamish. But then Hamish always attracted that limpet type of female, thought Priscilla sourly.

John Taylor moved around to the far side of the cloth to put a distance between himself and the glutton. But when Peta began to eat, he realized his mistake. He had a perfect view of all that gorging and stuffing. If she would only eat silently, he thought, it would not be so bad. But she snorted and chomped and breathed heavily through her nose.

'Where's Crystal?' asked Priscilla, wondering if she could slow Peta down by engaging her in conversation.

'Asleep, probably,' said Peta through spray of breadcrumbs. 'Very fond of me, she is. Doesn't like her parents much and I can't say I blame her. Pair of old bores.'

'That does not say very much for her,' snapped John. 'Children should honour and obey their parents.'

'You must have come out of the ark, sweetie,' said Peta and then roared with laughter. 'You should be a judge. You know,

46

one of those ones who live in the Dark Ages and says things like, "What does the witness mean by *heavy metal music*"?'

And John, who did not know what heavy metal was but had no intention of betraying the fact, said instead, 'You have not been very well brought up, Mrs Gore, or rather, that is my impression.'

'Wine, anyone?' said Priscilla desperately.

'Oh, what makes you think that?' Peta batted her eyelashes at him. 'I know. You think I am a terrible flirt.'

'You are indeed a *terrible* flirt,' he said in his dry, precise voice, 'in that you have no delicacy of manner. Your eating habits are disgusting.'

They all held their breath. But Peta had noticed a spare salmon steak and that was enough to make her temporarily deaf. She reached out and picked it up with her fingers. It began to disintegrate, but she hurriedly crammed it into her mouth. Then she seized the table-cloth to wipe her hands and everyone's glasses of wine went flying.

Jessica Fitt found that the very sight of Peta made her feel physically ill. She liked her life to be well ordered. She liked beautiful flowers and beautiful paintings. She did not bother much about the sort of clothes she put on because, like most women of low self-esteem, she did not consider herself worth embellishing.

'Are you all right?' she heard Peter Trumpington ask.

47

'I'm sorry,' she said. 'I shouldn't let her get to me. But this'—she waved a hand around the white sandy beach to the clear blue sea—'it's so perfect, so beautiful, and there she sits in the middle of it like a great pile of excrement.'

'You mean the Peta woman?'

'Yes.'

'Would you like to know what to do about her?'

'There's nothing up with her that a well-thrown hand-grenade wouldn't cure.'

'Come on, Jessica. Spare me. Look at the size of her. There'd be bits of her splattered from here to America. Can you imagine bits of Peta raining down on New York City?'

Jessica stifled a sudden giggle. 'What would you do, Peter?'

He leaned behind him and pulled a bottle of white wine out of the crate and then picked up a corkscrew. 'I'd get drunk,' he said. 'Let's get through this bottle before she gets to it.'

Something sad and repressed and rigid inside Jessica seemed to melt. She laughed and held out her glass. 'Here's to sanity,' she said.

'Have you ever thought of committing a crime?' John asked Jenny. His panama hat was pulled down over his face so she could not see the expression in his eyes.

'Well, no, I don't think so. I feel like killing *her*.' She waved a hand in Peta's direction. 'But I mean, it's just a thought. But you don't mean murder, do you? Do you mean theft or arson or

48

shop-lifting?'

'I have dealt with so many criminals,' he said in a tired voice. 'Very few of them show any remorse. They are angry at getting caught out, that's all. They go to prison and the taxpayer has to pay for their keep.'

'You don't mean you want to see hanging brought back?'

'Why not? Why should we work and slave all our lives to keep them cosseted in jails, to keep them fed, to pay for prisoners' rehabilitation, to pay for therapists?'

'I suppose you have a point,' said Jenny diplomatically. She looked longingly in the direction of Hamish Macbeth, but he had gone to sleep. 'Priscilla's about to dish out the fresh fruit salad,' she said. 'I must help her.'

'Go ahead,' he said wearily. 'I'm going for a walk.'

'But you'll miss dessert!'

'I'll miss the sight of that swine eating it!'

He turned and strode off.

The castle cook, perhaps to ease his conscience, as he had probably decided before preparing the lunch not to go, had made enough fruit salad for twenty, and Peta ate most of it. No one else was hungry. Jessica Fitt and Peter Trumpington were drinking steadily and whispering to each other, snorting with laughter and then looking furtively around like bad children. They were vying with each other over the best way to kill Peta.

49

At last, gorged with food, Peta fell asleep. She lay on her back with her mouth open, snoring. Maria thought, she's going to get a horrendous sunburn, but she did not move. Let her get burnt, and with luck burnt so badly that it puts her out of commission for the rest of the week.

With Peta asleep, a relaxed air took hold of the party. John returned from his walk in time to join in the general, lazy conversation. Seagulls swooped and dived for scraps of food.

'Do you remember that film, I forget the one, but where they killed this chap by tying him into a rowing-boat and then tied a fish on his head? The cormorants dived for the fish and split his skull open.'

'What made you think of a gruesome thing like that?' asked Priscilla.

'Oh, nothing,' said Peter and nudged Jessica, who laughed immoderately and then held out her glass for more wine.

Priscilla applied sun-barrier lotion to her face and arms and then, with a casual familiarity which grated on Jenny, she walked over to the sleeping Hamish Macbeth and started gently putting lotion on his face and arms. Hamish stirred in his sleep and smiled.

When she had finished, Priscilla said, 'Well, we should think about getting back. Want to help me put the stuff away, Jenny?'

'Do it yourself,' said Jenny. 'That's your

50

job,' and then blushed scarlet and got up and walked away.

Damn Hamish, thought Priscilla. She poked him in the ribs. 'Wake up. Help me with this stuff.'

Hamish sleepily struggled up. 'Where's my helper?'

'If you mean Jenny, she's gone off after reminding me sharply that packing up is my job. The shy clinging kind certainly go for you, Hamish, and you do nothing to discourage it.'

'Why should I?' he said maliciously. 'She's a fine-looking girl. Talent's a bit thin on the ground in Lochdubh.'

'You having already run through most of it!' Priscilla began to rattle dishes with unnecessary force. Jenny came back, muttered 'Sorry,' and began to help.

Once back on board, Mary French decided to show off her organizing skills by getting them to sing a round song. 'You first,' she ordered, as if dealing with a class of backward children. 'Then you.'

'Just like Joyce Grenfell,' said Peter and Jessica shrieked with laughter, then found she couldn't stop laughing and ended by bursting into tears.

The boat began to bucket up and down again as it approached the point of land which sheltered the sea loch of Lochdubh.

Priscilla had just produced afternoon tea— hot scones with Cornish cream and strawberry

51

jam—and spread it on the deck when Peta was suddenly and violently sick over it. Horrified, the rest backed off to the sides while Peta vomited and vomited. A normal person would soon have been reduced to dry heaving, but Peta had a capacious and overloaded stomach. The clients of Checkmate fled to the bow and huddled together, even Jenny, until they were joined by Priscilla and Maria.

'I can't take it,' said Maria with her handkerchief to her mouth. 'Hamish'll need to cope.'

They all stayed there until the *Jaunty Lass* edged into Lochdubh harbour.

Still they stayed until they saw Peta being helped ashore. With a sigh of relief, they saw Hamish talking to one of the locals, who had a small pick-up truck, and then he helped Peta into the back of it.

They edged round to get off the boat. The decks were clean, glistening with water.

Hamish appeared on board again.

'Brave man,' said Priscilla. 'Did you stack the stuff downstairs?'

'No,' said Hamish. 'I just tied the lot up in the table-cloth and threw it over the side.'

*   *   *

Hamish thought he never wanted to see anyone being sick again, but he found a couple of fishermen outside the local bar that evening

52

being violently ill. It turned out that Archie was regaling the locals inside with such a colourful story of his day out that Peta's sickness was more horrible in the telling than the actuality.

He walked on. A new restaurant, run by a Scottish-Italian family, had just opened on the waterfront. He heard the hum of voices from inside and was glad to see it was doing a good trade. He looked in the window and grinned.

The members of Checkmate had escaped and were enjoying dinner on their own. They were seated round a large table, talking and laughing. He felt sorry for Maria. But surely Peta would not be up to eating any more that day.

*　　*　　*

But Peta was working her way steadily through the dinner that had been meant for the whole party while Maria looked on with horrified loathing. She wondered why Crystal, who was lazily picking at her own food, was unaffected by her aunt's behaviour. Once the horrible meal was over, Maria plucked up her courage and followed Peta up to her room.

'Let's get down to business,' said Maria firmly, 'or what's left of it. Peta, you have succeeded in driving our clients away. They approached me and said they could not sit through another meal with you and I had to arrange dinner for them at a restaurant in the village.'

'Any good?'

'What?'

'The restaurant.'

'Never mind that! Listen to me. I want to buy you out.'

'No need for that. I'm an asset, Maria. And don't give me that rubbish about them dining elsewhere because of me. You arranged it. And do you know why?'

'No, do tell me, Peta, darling.'

'It's because you're jealous of me. You know I've got a way with the fellows and you're jealous.'

'And you're mad!' shouted Maria, her temper snapping. 'And hear this! If I've got to kill you to get rid of you, then by God I'll do it!'

Jenkins, the maître d'hôtel, who had been walking along the corridor outside, stopped and listened to this with interest before going on downstairs to irritate Mr Johnson by telling him that if one allowed common-type people into the hotel, then murder would be done, and mark his words!

* * *

Jenny Trask woke with a cry during the night and sat up in bed, her heart palpitating. She had just had a terrible dream in which Peta's dead body had been carried into the hotel

54

dining-room by Hamish Macbeth, who smiled at her and said, 'Roasted to a turn,' and then he had stuffed an orange in Peta's mouth before picking up the carving knife.

The room was stuffy. She got up and opened the window wide and leaned out. Then she gasped, staring at the mountains beyond. A great dark shadow was creeping down the mountains and sliding towards the castle, blotting out everything in its path. Then she realized it was only the shadow of a cloud crossing the moon and drew back with a nervous laugh. But the fear caused by that shadow would not go away. There was something sinister and evil approaching the castle, and no amount of logical thought would seem to make the fear go away.

CHAPTER THREE

*Some men there are that love not a gaping
     pig;*
Some, that are mad if they behold a cat.
                                    —SHAKESPEARE

Ian Chisholm, the driver of the minibus, was
there an hour earlier than had been originally
scheduled in response to an appeal from
Maria, Maria who was desperate to get her
charges out of the hotel before Peta joined
them.

The original plan had been to take them on a
tour of the surrounding countryside, returning
to the hotel for lunch, back out in the
afternoon, and then return for dinner.

Now she planned to keep them out until late
evening. They would go to Ullapool, have
lunch there, and then travel to the famous
Inverewe Gardens for the afternoon and have
dinner at some restaurant or hotel that did not
contain Peta. Priscilla came out to see them off,
a frown marring the perfection of her face. The
other guests were eating at any other
establishment but the Tommel Castle Hotel
and had complained to the colonel that
although the food was excellent, the sight of
Peta was putting them off. The colonel had
retaliated by blaming Mr Johnson and Priscilla

for having Checkmate as guests in the first place, and he was leaving with his wife that morning to visit friends in Caithness and said he would not return until Peta and Checkmate had left. Priscilla planned to turn one of the smaller hotel lounges, not often used, into a dining-room for Peta to dine alone with her niece, in the hope of luring some diners back. Tommel Castle stood to lose a sizeable sum of revenue if everyone decided to eat elsewhere.

The weather was still sunny, but there was a brassiness about it and the air had become close and humid. Sean, the cook, was fuming about Peta and planned to go down to the village after breakfast was served, and Priscilla did so hope he did not plan to get drunk.

Maria was telling the startled driver, Ian Chisholm, that the large fee he was getting from her meant he had to act as a guide as well. Like most of the natives, he knew very little of the history of Sutherland, but being a true Highlander, he planned to make it up as he went along.

When they were all on board the bus, Maria fairly yelled at Ian to get moving *fast* and heaved a sigh of relief as the bus rolled out onto the road without any sign of Peta in pursuit.

They had travelled quite a way south when Maria realized Ian was not doing his job. That is, he had not uttered a word. She saw the romantic ruin of a castle coming up on the right and called to Ian to stop and then, with a steely glint in her eye, said, 'Tell us about it.'

'Oh, Barren Castle,' said Ian, who had not the faintest idea what the building was or what it had been. 'That was the home of the Crummet family. They was supporters of Bonnie Prince Charlie and the redcoats were sure they had been sheltering the prince and tried to drive them off. But the laird said he would never leave, so them bastard redcoats burnt the castle ower his head. The family all perished, yea, and their oxen and cattle, too,' added Ian, who was a regular church attender. 'It's said his daughter, Fiona, still haunts the ruins.'

'Gosh!' said Deborah, struggling to the door of the bus with her camera at the ready. 'Must get a picture.'

The rest of them followed her but soon quickly retreated to the shelter of the bus, for the midges, those Scottish mosquitoes, had descended in droves. 'I forgot to bring repellent,' mourned Maria.

'I haff it here,' said Ian triumphantly. 'Three pounds a stick.' It had cost him one pound and fifty pence a stick in Patel's store in Lochdubh, but he felt his foresight deserved a profit. The bus then rumbled on, with Ian occasionally making up a story about some feature of the passing landscape.

Maria began to relax. It was all very sad and annoying about Peta. She had been such a jolly and likeable woman in the past. She had

58

enjoyed her food, but in reasonable quantities. But gradually she had begun to stuff herself, and the more she stuffed, the more her personality had undergone a change, becoming a mixture of vanity, arrogance, and bad temper. It was as if, thought Maria, food were some sort of mind-altering drug. Maybe it was. She had read somewhere something about Overeaters Anonymous. But it was the fashion to psychoanalyse people these days and it was all so tiresome and irritating, as if one could no longer be allowed the luxury of disliking someone. If Peta had a problem about food, then it was Peta's job to do something about it.

There was no doubt, thought Maria with feeling, that Peta's perpetual interference in the business was beginning to affect her, Maria's, judgement. Take this lot, she thought, twisting her neck round to look at them. Who would have thought of such unlikely combinations? No—she gave herself a mental shake—she was not losing her grip, Peta or no Peta. It was something to do with this weird place and landscape. Introduce the same bunch of people to each other at a London cocktail party and they would not have paired off in the same way.

* * *

Sean, the cook, shouldered his way into the bar in Lochdubh, which opened early to cater for the fishermen. He was not in the best of moods, to say the least, and the ribbing he got from the customers about 'thon great fat wumman up at the castle' made his temper worse.

'All ma art gone bust,' he said in a strong Glasgow accent. 'I could put shite down in front o' that bitch and she would shovel it down. I could get her to eat anything.'

Archie Maclean's eyes gleamed with mischief. 'Could ye get her to eat this? Dougie brought it in. He didnae shoot it. Found it dead. Died o' auld age if you ask me.' He opened a sack and dragged out a dead wild cat, a great beast with mangy-looking fur. From the rank smell of it, it had been dead several days.

'Course,' sneered Sean. 'Told you I could get her tae eat anything.'

Archie winked at the others. 'Put your money where your mouth is, Sean.'

'Whit?'

'Serve this cat up tae her the night and if she eats the lot, I'll pay ye ten pound.'

The others began to press their bets.

'I'll dae it,' said Sean. He shoved the cat back in the sack and then heaved the sack over his shoulder.

'Hey, wait a bit,' said one of the fishermen. 'And how is we tae know whether the fat wumman ate it or no'?'

'Archie here can come up and sit in the

dining-room,' said Sean. 'She's frightened the other guests awa', so nobody'll notice.'

*   *   *

The clients of Checkmate strolled along the waterfront at Ullapool, scrubbing their faces with sticks of repellent. Ullapool is the home of a particularly savage tribe of midges. But it is a beautiful little town with a pretty harbour and some good shops. Despite the heat and the midges, everyone was in a good mood, and even John Taylor walked with a jaunty step.

Lunch in a waterfront restaurant was not particularly good, being of the chips-with-everything variety, but Peta was not there and the sun was still shining and there seemed a determination on everyone's part to enjoy the day. They talked incessantly of Peta and how horrible she was, still drawn together by that communal resentment, until Maria began to realize what Priscilla had already guessed: Peta, in her repulsive way, was an asset.

They made their way after lunch to Inverewe Gardens which, despite the fact that they are in the far north of Britain, are near the Gulf Stream and so boast palm trees and many exotic plants.

Maria deliberately let them think they were all returning to the castle for dinner, because when the gaiety of the group began to flag, she announced they were stopping for dinner somewhere on the road home and so the spirits of everyone soared again at this further reprieve from Peta.

The dinner at an unpretentious hotel recommended by Priscilla was simple but good. The company enlivened the evening by picturing Peta wolfing down her solitary dinner.

*   *   *

And it was a solitary dinner, too. Peta had trailed around all day, feeling cross that the others had escaped her. A large breakfast and larger lunch did nothing to restore her mood. Crystal, who should have been some sort of a companion, had passed the day in her room, reading magazines and doing things to her hair and nails. Peta called on her to ask her to come downstairs for dinner but met with a rebuff. Crystal's hair was in rollers and she said she was trying out a new style and wasn't going to take them out. She said she was going to have a flask of coffee and some sandwiches in her room. Peta began to protest loudly, saying as she was paying for Crystal's holiday in this expensive hotel, then the least Crystal could do was to keep her company. But Crystal had a genius for turning suddenly deaf. All the while her aunt was railing at her, she lazily flipped over the pages of a film magazine and did not appear to hear a word.

62

Peta hated her own company. Almost tearfully, she ended up by saying, 'You were the sole beneficiary in my will but the first thing I'm going to do when I get back to London is cut you out.'

Crystal did hear that. She thought briefly about following Peta downstairs and making amends, but that would mean taking the rollers out of her hair. She picked up the magazine again.

Priscilla ushered Peta into the dining-room. There had been no reason to turn another room into a separate dining-room, for no one else was eating at the hotel that evening. Peta looked so downcast that Priscilla said that the cook was preparing a special meal for her, as she was the only diner. Priscilla was relieved that Sean had returned from the village sober and in such good spirits and prepared to create something for Peta.

In the kitchen, Sean looked down at his handiwork with satisfaction. He had skinned the cat and stewed it gently for hours in a rich wine sauce embellished with mushrooms and herbs. Before it, he planned to serve only a thin consommé, not wanting to spoil the glutton's appetite.

Peta drank the soup and eagerly waited for this special main course. The waitress brought it in in a large casserole. Peta's eyes gleamed. 'Leave it,' she said. 'I'll serve myself.'

She got through the lot, along with a

63

mountain of sautéed potatoes and a dish of cauliflower and cheese and then leaned back and wiped her mouth with her napkin and gave a satisfied belch. 'Bring the cook here,' she said grandly to the waitress. 'I wish to compliment him.'

As Sean entered the dining-room, he whispered to the waitress, 'Run along. I've left a glass of wine for you in the kitchen.'

Then he approached Peta and smiled in triumph as he saw the empty casserole.

'That was excellent,' said Peta. 'But what was it? Venison?'

Sean smiled insolently down at her. 'Cat,' he said. Archie Maclean, who had crept quietly into the dining-room, stared at them. Peta blinked at Sean. 'You surely didn't say "cat."'

'Aye, cat, moggie, pussie ... C-A-T. I bet the boys in the bar that you waud eat anything, and so you did. One auld smelly wild cat.'

'Get the manager,' spluttered Peta, turning green. 'You're mad.'

'Oh, no, you fat pig,' hissed Sean, leaning over her with a courteous smile pinned on his face in case anyone looked in the dining-room door. 'You say one word, and ah'll take the meat cleaver through your fat neck. But you won't. You do and ah'll phone the newspapers and say ah served you the beast to teach a snorting, guzzling pig like you a lesson.'

He turned and stalked off and Archie slid out after him.

64

Peta got shakily to her feet, her handkerchief jammed against her mouth. She ran all the way to her room, where she was very sick indeed. She would need to leave, need to get away. It was awful, horrible. Just because she enjoyed her food that madman had threatened her. She would call on that nice policeman. She was almost ready to go to look for Hamish Macbeth when she sat down again with a groan. What if it got in the newspapers? Maria would claim that she was ruining the business. Everywhere she went, people would watch her eating. Peta snuffled dismally.

It was all Maria's fault. Maria must have been spreading tales about her. Yes, Maria was jealous and had no doubt paid the cook to drive her away. So she wasn't going. She was going to stay and snatch up one of these men and teach Maria a lesson.

*   *   *

Priscilla received a phone call from Hamish Macbeth. He sounded worried. He said he was on his way up to the castle to talk to her.

Soon she heard the police Land Rover skidding to a halt outside the castle. She went out to meet Hamish.

'Where's Peta Gore?' he asked.

'In her room.'

'Well, I hope she's all right. I saw Sean rushing into the bar and followed him in and

65

listened. He was collecting bets. They didn't see me at first, so I was able to learn that Sean had cooked up some old wild cat and served it to Peta, who ate it for dinner.'

'He's run mad,' gasped Priscilla. 'Let's hope she never finds out. I'd better tell Johnson to fire Sean, although where we're going to get another cook in the middle of the season, I don't know.'

'It's worse than that. He *did* tell her.'

'We'll have the press on the doorstep in the morning. We'll be ruined,' wailed Priscilla.

'Aye, but maybe we can keep it quiet. Look, there was one thing that struck me about Peta. She fair fancies herself with the fellows. You'd best take me up to her. Leave the whole thing to me. You can keep Sean for the summer if I can arrange everything and then get rid of him when things quieten down. Tell Johnson to start now looking for another chef but don't tell him why.'

'But the locals...'

'Oh, them,' said Hamish. 'I can get that lot to shut up any time. Now lead me to Peta.'

Priscilla took him up the stairs and knocked at Peta's door. A faint voice called, 'Come in.'

'Do your stuff, Hamish, but God knows how you're going to manage it,' said Priscilla.

Hamish went into Peta's bedroom and closed the door behind him. Priscilla waited, irresolute, and then went off down the stairs.

'What do you want?' Peta asked the tall

66

constable who stood humbly before her, his cap under his arm.

'I came to see if you were all right,' said Hamish. 'I gather the mad cook served you a venison casserole and told you it was cat.'

'Venison...?'

'Aye, you see he made this daft bet with the locals that he could get anyone to eat anything and so they gave him an old wild cat. Not wanting to lose his money, he pretended to you that it was cat, although he actually made it from the best haunch of venison. The trouble is, I gather, he was insulting and threatening.'

'He was indeed!'

'Aye, well, there he was telling the others that that wass the only thing he wass ashamed of,' said Hamish, his accent growing more sibilant, as it usually did when he was upset or embarked on a really stupendous lie. 'As a matter of fact, he wass telling them that he fair fancied you himself. That wass what wass so disgusting.'

Peta glanced in the mirror and tweaked a curl into place. 'Of course,' went on Hamish, 'I am sure you would rather leave and sue the hotel for the indignity of it all. Mind you, it's the silly season and these things haff a way of getting into the newspapers...'

'Oh, I wouldn't want that,' said Peta hurriedly. She wanted this nice policeman to go on telling her about how the cook actually fancied her. Her subconscious was grasping that there was a way out of facing up to the fact that she was a compulsive overeater in the way that an alcoholic will blame the coffee and marmalade at breakfast or anything else as a reason for his chronic diarrhoea. Anything is to blame but drink. And in Peta's case, anything but food.

'In fact, the silly loon was chust saying about how pretty you wass,' said Hamish, laying it on with a trowel.

'You men,' said Peta. 'I don't understand you.'

'I don't understand the behaviour of some men myself,' said Hamish severely. 'They will go to cruel lengths to attract the attention of some lady, even to the extent of threatening her. The point is this: If Sean apologizes to you, will you let the whole matter drop?'

Peta chewed one chubby thumb and glanced up at the constable. She longed to sue the hotel, or at least get Tommel Castle to pay her something for the indignity. But if she did that, the whole thing might come out, including the fact that she had been gullible enough to think that delicious meal was old wild cat. The newspapers would have a field day.

'I have been sick,' she said. 'Very sick and frightened, too.'

'Chust let Sean come and apologize to you. A great lady like yourself can surely accept an apology,' said Hamish humbly.

'Very well,' said Peta. She glanced in the
68

mirror again. 'Goodness, I look a fright.'

As Hamish left, she was reaching for her bag of cosmetics.

'So far so good,' said Hamish to Priscilla. 'She's prepared to let the matter drop if Sean apologizes. Quick, go into the office and get me his file.'

Once he had the file in his possession, he flicked through it. 'Check any of this?' he asked.

'Mr Johnson's supposed to do that,' said Priscilla, 'but you know how it is up here. You get so desperate for good staff, you don't care too much about checking up on them.'

Hamish left her and drove quickly down to Lochdubh. Why should such an excellent chef as Sean come all the way to the north of Scotland? He was a townee. He was always making disparaging remarks about Highlanders. So, with any luck, he had a criminal record. No time to check. The longer Peta was left alone, the more she would realize that the tale he had spun her was absolutely ridiculous.

He went straight to the bar and took away the glass that Sean was about to raise to his lips. He faced the others. 'If any word of what this fool has been telling you gets out, I will sue the lot of you for slander. Come with me, Sean. You're in bad trouble.'

'I suppose ah'm fired,' said Sean sulkily as Hamish led him outside.

69

'Not yet. Now listen, you daft gowk. I know you have a criminal record.'

Sean stared at the ground. 'You have even done a prison term for assault.'

'A man's got a right to knock his wife about,' muttered Sean.

Thank God for Highland intuition, thought Hamish. 'Look, Sean, I can get you off the hook; otherwise you'll be down in prison in Strathbane tomorrow morning.'

Sean looked at him pleadingly. 'Ah'm an artist,' he said. 'That wumman is mair than flesh and blood can stand.'

'Well, you're going to have to stand it. You've got to come back with me and apologize to her and tell her it was a venison casserole, and what's more, you've got to let her think you fancy her.'

'That great scunner. Aw, go and bile yer heid, Hamish!'

'The only alternative is prison, and I'll make sure you get a long stretch.'

Sean stared wildly around. It was still light, for there are only a few hours of semi-darkness in a Highland summer. A pale-green sky stretched across the glassy loch. The air smelled sweetly of peat smoke, for fires were lit even in the hot weather to heat water for washing. A man was rowing out into the bay, phosphorescence from the water dripping like jewels from his oars. A gull was picking its way gingerly along the shore over the oily rocks and

70

glistening seaweed.

Unbalanced as he was, Sean had come to love Lochdubh, although not for one minute would he admit it to anyone. He gave a broken little sigh. 'All right, ah'll do it, Hamish. But if there was one way of removing that fat wumman frae this planet and not get caught fur it, I would do it, and gladly, too.'

They drove in silence to the castle. 'There's the others,' said Hamish, seeing the minibus in front of them on the narrow road. He leaned on the horn. Ian stopped in a lay-by and Hamish shot past and disappeared up the drive to the castle in a cloud of dust.

'Don't leave me,' pleaded Sean when they were outside Peta's door.

'No, I'm staying with you,' said Hamish. 'In you go.'

Peta was reclining in bed. Her face was heavily made up and she was wearing a pink negligee which clashed with her red hair.

Sean sank to his knees on the carpet and babbled out a stammering apology with all the histrionic overacting of the Glasgow drunk which Hamish began to feel might go on forever and Sean hadn't got to the bit about fancying her. He kicked him with his boot.

'And tae say all them awful things to a lady as fine and beautiful as yerself,' mourned Sean. 'Ah'll never raise my head again.'

Peta smiled slowly and her recently emptied stomach rumbled. 'Well, I'm still a teensy bit

71

peckish, so if you'll just whip me up an omelette or something, I'll forgive you.'

Hamish jerked Sean to his feet. 'Good idea,' he said heartily.

Half an hour later, Peta had consumed a twelve-egg ham omelette with a mound of chipped potatoes and was feeling quite elated. Priscilla had presented her with a bottle of champagne. Priscilla had told Mr Johnson that Peta wrote a column on hotels and restaurants for a glossy magazine and that the staff were to be instructed to be extra attentive to her. She also awarded a thousand-pound prize annually, said Priscilla, to the best hotel servant.

Priscilla then felt uneasily that Hamish Macbeth's facility for lying was rubbing off on her. She walked out with him to the Land Rover.

'I can't begin to tell you how very grateful I am to you,' said Priscilla. 'Do you think it's safe to have Sean around now?'

'I think he'll behave himself,' said Hamish. 'The man's a marvellous cook. It's because he's a wee runt from Glasgow that his eccentricities seem so sinister. If he worked in a famous French restaurant, he would be regarded as a great character.'

Priscilla held out her hand. 'Anyway, thanks a lot, Hamish.'

His hazel eyes glinted down at her in the twilight. 'What about a kiss?'

72

'Oh, *Hamish*.' She smiled and raised her head to kiss him on the cheek but he twisted his head and his lips came down on hers, gentle and warm.

The kiss was very brief but Priscilla felt oddly shaken. Hamish stared at her angrily for a moment and then said abruptly, 'Call me if there's any more trouble.'

Priscilla stood and watched him go. He drove off very quickly and did not acknowledge her wave.

'Damn,' muttered Hamish, staring bleakly through the windscreen. 'Why the hell did I do that? I don't want to have to live through all that nonsense again.'

*   *   *

Maria noticed that they were being served breakfast the next morning in a dining-room separate from the other guests. All Peta's fault. And yet the hotel staff were treating Peta like a queen and the chef had come into the dining-room twice to ask her humbly if there was anything special he could cook for her. Peta was smiling and beaming with all this attention. She ate surprisingly moderately for her and it soon dawned on Maria that men were now the focus of Peta's desires. She flirted with Sir Bernard and John Taylor. Her flirtation took the line of rather old-fashioned bawdy jokes about what the bishop had said to

73

the actress. Only Crystal laughed. Crystal, too, was being very attentive to her aunt. Her new hair-style made her look as if she had been caught in a high gale, but her somewhat characterless face was as fashionably beautiful as ever. She was wearing very brief shorts with high-heeled sandals.

Maria, regretting that the pre-arranged programme meant that the party could not get off early and escape Peta, rose to her feet. 'You will see from your programmes,' she said, 'that we are planning a visit to the theatre in Strathbane this afternoon, although we will leave late in the morning and have a packed lunch on the bus. It is a Scottish comedy show and I hope you will all enjoy it.'

'Will the theatre be air-conditioned?' asked Sir Bernard, who was already sweating in the close heat.

'I doubt it. I don't even know a London theatre that's air-conditioned.'

Mr Johnson came in with a fax and handed it to Peta. She read it. 'It's from my accountant,' she said, beaming all round. 'Do you know, Maria, I am now worth three million.'

'Three million *pounds*,' exclaimed Sir Bernard.

'Exactly,' said Peta.

'But that's extraordinary. Surely a share in a matrimonial agency can't bring in that sort of revenue.'

'No, sweetie, a rich husband who left me the

74

lot and a good stockbroker.'

Sir Bernard gave her a calculating look. Three million. He was rich, but never too rich not to want more. He could expand his business with a dowry like that. And with the way she ate, she wouldn't live long.

John Taylor felt shaken. He'd always thought of men having a lot of money, but not women. Peta was surely nearly past the age of child-bearing. She must be ... what ... forty-five? And yet, three million. If he married her, that three million would become his, or rather, he would see to that. Then what would his son and daughter think when he died and left the lot elsewhere? Of course, the full impact would be spoilt if he died before Peta, but she couldn't live long. That bulk of hers must be a terrible strain on the heart.

Three million, thought Matthew Cowper. I could buy a stately home with that and entertain the chairman and his wife and see their eyes pop out. I could have a Rolls to drive to work. Dammit, I could have a chauffeur. Peta looked a freak. But being married to a freak in a stately home was different from being married to a freak in a small bungalow. She would be considered Falstaffian and eccentric.

Of the men, only Peter Trumpington remained unmoved.

This is awful, thought Jenny Trask. Those men are all looking at her in such a horribly calculating way. They're all rich. Well, Matthew Cowper, I gather, has simply got a good salary, but greed is stamped on their faces. In fact, we're all greedy in one way—for romance, for money, for love. I wish Peta hadn't said that about her millions. Deborah, Jessica, and Mary are looking as if they could kill her.

Crystal was leaning back in her chair, her cloud of artistically tangled hair shielding her expression. Jenny wondered what she was thinking and whether she had accompanied her aunt to the Highlands with a view to becoming Peta's legatee. As they rose to go, however, Crystal said languidly that she had a lot of things to do and would not be going with them.

On the bus there was a scramble by Matthew, John, and Sir Bernard to sit next to Peta. Matthew, being the youngest and most agile, got there first.

But at the theatre, it was John who succeeded in manoeuvring himself into a seat next to Peta by dint of buying her a large box of chocolates. The party were not all seated together, the seats being in twos throughout the auditorium. The noisy Scottish show ran its course, finishing up with a chorus line of small Scottish girls kicking their height in short tartan kilts to the wheezy music of the Strathbane Workers' Pipe Band.

Sir Bernard managed to secure the seat next

to Peta on the journey home. Deborah sat next to Jenny in silence. She had lost her exuberant spirits. Only Peter Trumpington and Jessica Fitt seemed happy as they sat together at the back, an odd couple, the handsome man and the grey woman.

Maria found her hands were shaking. Peta had probably arranged for that fax to arrive. The week was turning out a total disaster.

If only Peta would die.

That evening at dinner, Peta again ate very little and cracked jokes, and John and Matthew and Sir Bernard seemed to be vying with each other as to who could laugh the loudest.

After dinner, at nine o'clock, Peta suddenly announced she was going up to bed, and Crystal, like a beautiful shadow, followed her out. Deborah was not talking to Sir Bernard. She said she was going out for a walk. Mary French said something nasty about yuppies and said she had found the castle library and was going to retire there, books being better than men any time. John Taylor said he was going to bed. He was old and the day had been exhausting. Matthew went out for a walk, remarking that the light nights meant one could take a walk any hour of the day. Sir Bernard said he would accompany him and Matthew said nastily he preferred his own company, so Sir Bernard set out to go for a walk on his own.

Jenny asked Priscilla if she could borrow one of the castle cars. 'Of course,' said Priscilla. 'Come into the office, I have to take the number of your driving licence before you go.'

Once she had written down the number, Priscilla said, 'You'll find the keys in the ignition. Car theft is one crime that hasn't reached Lochdubh yet. Where are you going?'

'Just a drive down to the village.'

'Going to visit anyone?' asked Priscilla sweetly.

'I don't know anyone,' snapped Jenny and walked off.

Half an hour later, Priscilla decided to run down to the village herself and call on Hamish Macbeth.

She drove to the police station. The hotel car was parked outside.

She swung the wheel and drove back to the castle.

Inside the police station, Jenny was saying earnestly, 'It must strike you as odd that I should join something like Checkmate.'

'I just thought it was the fashion these days.' Hamish heard a car driving up, stopping and then turning about and driving away. He was sure that it had been Priscilla and he looked at Jenny Trask with a certain amount of irritation in his eyes.

'I am a policeman, Miss Trask,' he said, 'and not used to being disturbed so late in the evening except on police work. I do have a

78

certain amount of chores to do before I go to bed. Did you come to see me about anything important?'

'I felt I had to see someone sane,' said Jenny, improvising wildly. Things were not turning out as she had expected. She had thought that Hamish might be intrigued by her visit. 'I wish I had never come up here. It's all so foreign and wild and weird. It gives me odd ideas.' She knew she was babbling on but somehow could not stop. 'The other night, I looked out and there seemed to be this great darkness approaching the castle. It turned out to be a cloud, but it gave me a creepy feeling. I went to the cinema once with a friend and no sooner had we sat down than I said to her, "Let's move. There's someone mad behind us." Well, it was pitch-black, for the movie had started, so my friend said it was nonsense. But a few moments later, this old woman behind us started muttering obscenities.'

Hamish looked at her, a sudden alertness in his eyes. 'So you think one of the party at the castle is mad?'

'There's something about it all that makes me uneasy,' said Jenny a trifle defiantly because this Highland policeman was making her feel like a fool.

'Why do you want to get married?' asked Hamish.

Jenny coloured up. 'Most people do, you know. I'm only a legal secretary. It's not as if I would be throwing up a great career to be a wife and mother.'

'Why not have a great career?' Hamish leaned back in his chair and clasped his hands behind his head.

'What?'

'Your family must have money, or Checkmate wouldn't have accepted you. So you could study for the bar. Take a law degree. My, my.' He half closed his eyes. 'I can see it all: Jenny Trask, Q.C., defender of the poor and oppressed.'

'I never even thought of it.' Jenny gave an awkward laugh. 'Me ... standing up in court! I'd be too shy.'

'I don't think you would be shy at all if you were defending someone, fighting for someone's innocence,' said Hamish.

She wrapped her legs round the kitchen stool she was sitting on and clasped the cup of coffee he had given her tightly to her bosom. She could see herself in wig and gown. She could see herself on television outside the Law Courts with a successfully acquitted celebrity beaming beside her.

'And now,' prompted Hamish gently, 'it's getting late, and so ...'

Jenny's mind came into land on reality and she blinked at him.

'Oh, yes, I must go. Thank you for the coffee.'

Hamish shook his head in amusement when

80

she had gone. He had given her a dream to chew over and he hoped that would keep her happy for the rest of the week.

He went outside to make sure he had locked up his hens for the night and then he walked down to the garden gate and looked out over the loch.

A sudden burst of wind came racing down the loch, setting the boats bobbing wildly, tearing among the rambling roses over the police-station door, whipping off the garbage-can lid, flying down Lochdubh and then disappearing as quickly as it had come.

The ripples on the loch subsided, the air grew close and still and a few stars burned feebly in the half-light of the sky.

He picked up the garbage-can lid and replaced it with automatic fingers. It was as if that wind had been racing towards Tommel Castle. He gave a superstitious shiver.

'Daft,' he chided himself as he went indoors, as daft as Jenny's imaginary mad people at the castle.

CHAPTER FOUR

Into the jaws of death,
Into the mouth of hell
—ALFRED, LORD TENNYSON

The landscape had lost its clear sharp colours when the party assembled outside the bus in the morning. They were due to go on a visit to a fish-farm, returning to the hotel for lunch and then a leisurely afternoon playing tennis or croquet in the grounds.

Crystal arrived at the bus despite the early hour. She was wearing a brief sun-suit which left little of her stupendous figure to the imagination. 'Auntie's not coming,' she volunteered. 'She's gone. She's left a note to say she's walked down to get the early-morning bus.'

The women looked relieved. 'Thank God,' muttered Maria.

Priscilla watched them all drive off, wondering uneasily whether Peta had had second thoughts about Sean's behaviour. She was joined by the hotel manager, Mr Johnson. 'Good riddance,' he said.

'Mrs Gore's up and gone,' said Priscilla.

'Oh, dear. I'd better tell Sean not to bother preparing lunch for her. I don't like that fat woman, but she's worked wonders on Sean. He does everything without complaint. I was even beginning to think she was an asset. Why don't you take some time off now that she's left? Your father's not here to pester us.'

'What about lunch?'

'The waitresses are all on duty. I'm here.'

Priscilla hesitated. Then she said, 'I might take a packed lunch and go off somewhere.'

Helped by Sean, who was almost servile, Priscilla packed a picnic hamper with enough for two, hoisted it into the Range Rover and drove down to the police station. Hamish was sitting in his front garden in a deckchair, reading the newspapers.

'I'm glad to see you've got the crime wave of Lochdubh subdued,' said Priscilla. 'If Detective Chief Inspector Blair could see you now!'

'Well, thon pest's safely in Spain. What brings you? Everything all right up at the castle?'

'Very much all right. Peta's gone. She left a note to say she was walking down to get the early-morning bus.'

Hamish slowly put down his newspaper. 'That's odd,' he said.

'What's odd? I mean, what can be so specially odd in the behaviour of a woman whose whole life-style is odd?'

'Well, she probably had heavy luggage...'

'Why? She didn't dress very well. A few baggy cotton dresses, things like that.'

83

'A glutton like her would have stashed away some goodies in her luggage, probably had whole hams and sides of beef in there.'

'Well, if she had, she'd have eaten them by now. What are you getting at?'

'For a fat woman like that with plenty of money to get up early and carry her suitcase down to the road to wait for the bus is verra strange. Also, if she was fed up, it would have been more in her nature to tell everyone off before she went. Then she would surely have said something to her niece.'

'You've been too long without crime,' said Priscilla with a laugh. 'She's gone and that's that. Would you like to come on a picnic with me, just somewhere up on the moors where we can get a bit of fresh air?'

'Love to. I'll just switch on the answering machine. And I'd best put my uniform in the car.'

'You're expecting trouble!'

'Just in case. I would hate to run into trouble and then the police from headquarters would come rushing up to find me without my uniform on.'

'It's this weather,' said Priscilla. 'It would give anyone odd ideas. It's so still and close; it feels threatening.'

*　　　*　　　*

When she returned to the hotel with the others,

84

Maria went straight up to Peta's room. There on the dressing-table was the note, type-written and unsigned. It said: 'Gone off to get the early-morning bus. Fed up with this place.'

Maria frowned down at it. Had something happened to irritate Peta? She opened the wardrobe and then the drawers. All her clothes were gone. She went into the bathroom. The first thing she saw was Peta's sponge-bag. It was a draw-string one and it was dangling by its strings from one of the taps. She unhitched it and opened it up. It contained deodorant, toothpaste, hairpins, and an expensive bar of soap. But Peta's tooth-brush was not there. She must have at least taken that. Puzzled and yet relieved at the same time, Maria carried it off with her. She could return it to Peta in London.

Jenny Trask sat on a deck-chair on the castle lawn. Things had settled down now that Peta was no longer with them. Mary French was teaching Matthew Cowper to play croquet, her high autocratic voice carrying to Jenny's ears. From the direction of the tennis courts came the sound of jolly laughter. Deborah was playing tennis with Sir Bernard. Peter Trumpington and Jessica Fitt were walking slowly together along by the flower-beds. Jenny felt a little stab of irritation. Peter certainly seemed a shallow young man without much in the way of intelligent conversation, but he was handsome and rich and it was

85

strange he appeared to feel so at home with the faded Jessica. Although she had little in the way of self-esteem, she did know that she was by far the best-looking female there, that is if one did not count Crystal, who was lying stretched out on the grass a little way away in a bikini of quite amazing brevity.

A shadow fell over Jenny and she looked up. John Taylor stood there, politely raising his hat. 'Mind if I join you?'

'Delighted,' said Jenny politely.

He drew a deck-chair up next to hers and sat down. 'Isn't it odd, Peta taking off the way she did,' said Jenny.

Unconsciously echoing Priscilla, John said, 'Everything about her was odd.'

'Maybe, but she was very vain ... goodness, I'm talking about the woman as if she were dead. I mean, she seemed to take a delight in riling and competing with Maria. I can't imagine her walking off without blaming someone first.'

'Perhaps this is her way of complaining,' said John lazily. 'Maria's looking worried, and that's probably the effect Peta meant to create.'

'But to leave without breakfast! Oh, well. At least this visit has got me thinking about a career.'

'In what way?' asked John. 'I thought the purpose of your coming here was matrimony.'

'It was. I'm grateful to Peta in a way because she has made the whole business of this dating

86

or marital agency distasteful. I'm thinking of taking my law exams.'

John looked at her in sudden dislike. 'And no doubt you will end up a judge. And do you know why?'

'No.'

'Because tokenism is slowly going to destroy the legal system of this country. Someone like you will be made a judge, not because of talent or brilliance or capability but simply because you are a woman. First it was the ethnic minorities, now it's bloody women.'

'I have not even started to study,' said Jenny in a thin voice, 'and yet you are prejudging my ability. Hardly a proper legal outlook.'

'Tcha!' said John and got up and walked angrily away.

Nasty man, thought Jenny, watching him go. Who is he to be so high and mighty? He was smarming around Peta at the theatre.

After a time, she rose and walked into the castle. Mr Johnson and Sean were standing by the reception. Sean was complaining that 'the fat wumman' had most certainly had breakfast; in fact, as far as he could tell, she had walked off with one of the castle picnic hampers and various goodies from the kitchen. Mr Johnson pointed out that Priscilla had packed and taken a picnic hamper, but Sean said he knew about that. She was probably off romancing that layabout of a policeman, he said.

87

Jenny walked on up to her room. So there was something between Priscilla and Hamish. And yet they must have known each other for some time and were not engaged.

She turned about and ran downstairs. Mr Johnson and Sean were still arguing. She interrupted them and asked Mr Johnson if she could take one of the castle cars.

'Let me see,' he said, 'Priscilla's got the Range Rover and Dougie borrowed the mini. The colonel's got his car. The old Volvo should be out front. You can have that. The keys are in the ignition.'

'I forgot to ask you before. Am I expected to pay for petrol?'

'Not if it's a short journey,' said Mr Johnson. 'But never leave the tank dry, always put back in what you use if you've been driving for a good distance. Have we got your driving-licence number?'

'Priscilla took a note of it last time.'

'That'll be all right then. But I wouldn't go too far today, if I were you. The weather looks bad.'

'There isn't a cloud in the sky!'

'The forecast's bad and there's a purple haze on the hills and that means thunder.'

Jenny got into the car and opened all the windows and the sun-roof. She drove quickly down to the police station, but there was no sign of Hamish. So he probably had gone off with Priscilla. She drove on to the harbour and

88

parked the car against the wall.

She was feeling hot and thirsty, so she went into the Lochdubh bar and ordered a gin and tonic and then wished she had not for the bar was full of men, not a woman in sight. 'How much is that?' she asked the barman.

'The chap down the end o' the bar's paid fur it.'

Jenny looked flustered. 'Who? What? I can't really...'

A tall young man in working clothes walked towards her. 'Sure, you looked as if you needed a drink,' he said. He had an engaging smile and a mop of black curls and blue, blue eyes.

'Did you pay for this?' asked Jenny.

'Yes, I always like to buy a pretty girl a drink. I'm working with Baxter's Forestry on the other side of the loch but we've packed it in for the day. One of the fellows dropped with heat exhaustion.'

Jenny felt herself relax. He seemed inoffensive and friendly. She finished her drink as they talked and then she bought the next round and somehow they found themselves sitting at one of the rickety bar tables telling each other their life stories. She forgot about Hamish Macbeth.

* * *

Hamish and Priscilla were having a late lunch. Hamish belonged unexpectedly to that

89

irritating breed who can never make up their minds where they want to choose to have a picnic, until Priscilla at last rebelled. She stopped after circling for quite some time round the narrow winding Highland roads at a spot on top of the moors where they could get a good view of both the castle and the surrounding countryside.

While they ate, Hamish went on and on about Peta's leaving, turning over the whys and wherefores until Priscilla said sharply, 'I'm bored with the very sound of that woman's name. Leave the subject alone, Hamish.'

His eyes mocked her. 'What would you like to talk about? Us?'

'Don't be silly.'

'What's so silly about it?' he asked, suddenly hell-bent on mischief. 'Here we are, a man and a woman, in the romantic Highlands of Scotland.'

'The Highlands of Scotland are only romantic to people who don't live in them,' said Priscilla, looking about for some way to change the subject. 'Look at those buzzards.'

Hamish twisted his head and shaded his eyes as he looked up at the sky. A pair of buzzards were circling lazily overhead a little distance away.

'Buzzards have the right idea,' he said, 'no marital agencies for them. Still thinking of joining Checkmate yourself, Priscilla?'

'Of course not. What's got into you,

Hamish? There's something ... uncomfortable about you.'

'If you want me to be comfortable, don't go around agreeing to kisses.'

'I only meant it to be a kiss on the cheek!'

'Oh, Priscilla.' He edged near her on the heather. She looked wide-eyed at him, her hands clenched. He put an arm about her shoulders and turned her face up to his.

A scream tore across the silence of the still landscape, a loud, frightened scream.

He jumped to his feet and stared around wildly. The scream was coming closer, now a thin whistling sound like an old-fashioned steam train heading for a tunnel.

Hamish ran out into the road. A small boy dragging a smaller boy behind him was running down the road, his mouth stretched by that horrible scream to its widest.

The boys collided into Hamish, the eldest throwing his arms around Hamish's knees.

'Quiet now,' said Hamish sternly and the scream stopped abruptly and the boy began to cry. Hamish prized him loose and knelt down and held him by the shoulders. He recognized the children as Jamie Ferguson and his little brother, Bill.

'Jamie, Jamie,' he said. 'It iss me. Hamish Macbeth. What iss it?'

'She's deid,' yelled Jamie and began to sob again.

'Where?' Hamish gave him a little shake.

'Ower there.' The boy pointed back the way he had come, in the direction of the circling buzzards. Priscilla had come up to join them.

'Look after this pair,' said Hamish to her. 'Give them some hot sweet tea. There's some left in the flask.'

He set off down the road at a run.

He knew every inch of the countryside and remembered that round the next turn, under the circling birds of prey, was a disused quarry which formed a small amphitheatre beside the road.

Hamish hurtled into the quarry, looking wildly about.

And then he saw a foot sticking out from behind a great boulder, a fat foot in a thin sandal, a foot with painted toe-nails.

He walked round the rock.

Peta Gore lay on her back, her sightless eyes staring up at the brassy sky. One large sandwich, half eaten, was clutched in one dead hand. But the most horrible thing, the ultimate indignity, was that a large red apple was crammed in her mouth.

He bent down and felt her pulse. He did it automatically, although he knew she was dead. He saw tyre tracks, faint in the dust of the quarry floor. Then he straightened and looked up at the sky. It was deepening in colour and a puff of damp breeze touched his cheek.

He ran back frantically to where Priscilla

was comforting the boys. 'It's Peta. She's dead,' he said. 'Get these boys down to Lochdubh, phone Strathbane, and then bring help back here. Get some of the men. Tell them to bring groundsheets and a tent. It's going to be a storm soon. Hurry! Oh, damn. My uniform.'

He grabbed his uniform out of the back of the Range Rover, tore off his casual clothes and changed into it while Priscilla, with quick efficient movements, cleared up the picnic and coaxed the shivering boys into the car.

Hamish ran back to where the body was lying, but this time he stood on guard outside the quarry, not wanting to tread on any clues. He flapped his arms at the buzzards above, only glad that they had not descended for dinner before the body was found.

The sky was turning milky white. The storm would appear to come down, he knew from experience, rather than blowing in from the west. The sky would deepen to grey and then black and then the rain would bucket down, blotting out any clues and those car tracks unless the men arrived first with the groundsheets.

*   *   *

Jenny Trask missed all the excitement when Priscilla burst into the bar, for she had already left with her forestry worker, Brian Mulligan.

93

They had drunk an awful lot and Jenny had taken him back to the castle bar, where they had drunk more. Looking through the door of the bar, Jenny had seen that the hall and reception desk were deserted, and so it had seemed like a good idea to slip Brian up to her room where eventually, between tangled sheets, the earth did seem to move for her as a most tremendous storm broke, rocking the castle to its foundations with peal after peal of thunder.

Outside, the Volvo, with windows open and sun-roof open, stood in the downpour and rain cascaded in, flooding the interior of the car.

* * *

Hamish stood in the pouring rain, shivering miserably. A tent had been erected over Peta's body and groundsheets covered a good deal of the floor of the quarry. Dr Brodie had examined the body and said he thought she had crammed the whole apple greedily into her mouth and had died of suffocation. Hamish shook his head slowly and said he'd be interested in what the police pathologist had to say.

Men from the village sat out in the road in their cars, passing round half-bottles of whisky and chatting excitedly.

And then the contingent from police headquarters arrived just as the storm-clouds

94

were rolling away and a bleak hellish light was beginning to illuminate the depressing scene.

To Hamish's dismay, first out of the cars was Detective Police Inspector Blair with his sidekicks, Harry Macnab and Jimmy Anderson.

Hamish stared at him stupidly. 'I thought you were in Spain!'

'Aye, well, ah'm back,' growled Blair. 'Stand aside, laddie, and let the experts get to it.'

The forensic team in white boiler suits were standing ready. The police pathologist went into the tent. Then he poked his head out of the flap and called, 'The rain's stopped. You can remove this.'

Several policemen removed the tent. A shaft of watery sunlight shone down, lighting up Peta's dead face.

'Jist like a roast pig,' said Blair with a laugh.

Dr Brodie moved forward. 'I was just saying to Macbeth here,' he said to the police pathologist, 'that this lady had the reputation of being a glutton. It was all over the village. She came here for a picnic and crammed an apple into her mouth and died of suffocation.'

'She died of suffocation all right,' said the pathologist, kneeling down by the body again.

To Blair's irritation, Hamish moved forward. He pointed a long finger to Peta's nostrils. 'See those little bruises,' said Hamish. 'I think someone rammed the apple in her mouth and pinched her nostrils tight so that

95

she would suffocate. It's a clear case of murder. She's lying on a patch of gravel but you can see where it's churned up about her feet where she writhed about.'

'Oh, for hivven's sakes,' moaned Blair. 'Waud ye leave the diagnosis tae the experts, you bampot.' The pathologist looked brightly up at Hamish, like an inquisitive bird. 'You know this woman, Macbeth?'

'Yes, Peta Gore is her name. She was partner in a marital agency called Checkmate who brought a party of their clients to Tommel Castle Hotel, where they still are. Although she's a partner, the firm is really run by a woman called Maria Worth, who had tried to keep the visit secret from Peta. Peta left a note this morning saying she was leaving, that she was walking down to catch the bus. But where are her clothes, where's her luggage? And she's a long way from the bus stop.'

The pathologist bent over the body again. 'You could be right,' he said. 'I mean, come to think of it, if she'd started to choke, she would have pulled the apple out of her mouth. If it's murder, it's a peculiarly vicious one. And I'll tell you something else. It isn't always possible to tell the exact time of death, but I would hazard a guess and say she died sometime last night.'

The groundsheets were being tenderly removed and a photographer was taking pictures of the tyre tracks. 'Very faint,' he said.

'Lucky you were here to get them covered, Macbeth.'

Blair glared at Hamish. Certainly Hamish had solved murders in the past and let Blair take the credit, but when Blair had been leaving headquarters, his super had said, 'Oh, well, if it's a murder, I'm sure Hamish will soon have an idea who did it.'

That had rankled. Worse, the super had referred to Macbeth as Hamish, a familiarity which Blair did not like.

Blair threw an arm around Hamish's shoulders. 'You're wet through, laddie,' he said. 'Why don't you run along to that polis station of yours an' dry off. Anderson here will run you down. Where's your car, by the way?'

Hamish had no intention of telling Blair that he had been picnicking on the moors with Priscilla when he was supposed to be on duty— not yet anyway.

'Two wee boys found the body,' he said. 'I got someone to drive them back.'

'Off you go wi' Anderson then. We'll call you when we need you.'

'You'd better,' said Hamish, 'or I'll need to put an independent report into Strathbane.' He walked off with Jimmy Anderson and left Blair staring after him.

'So what brought that old scunner back from Spain?' asked Hamish as Jimmy drove down into Lochdubh. The sky was clearing but a brisk wind had sprung up, ruffling the surface

97

of the loch. The golden days were over and someone had murdered Peta.

'He got drunk in a bar in one o' thae places on the Costa Brava and picked a fight wi' a Spaniard and ended up thumping him one. The Spaniard calls the police. Turns out the Spaniard is head honcho in the town. Blair protests he's a policeman, Spanish police say in that case he's more of a disgrace and if he disnae want to be booked, then he'd better get the next plane out.'

'Why, oh why didn't they arrest him?' mourned Hamish.

* * *

Mr Johnson, emerging from the castle after the storm, found the soaked Volvo. He got two of the maids and told them to dry and polish the soaked interior and then went to the reception desk where he noticed Jenny's key was missing, which meant she must be in her room.

He went upstairs and knocked loudly on her door. Jenny struggled awake, forgot there was someone in bed with her, and called, 'Come in!'

Mr Johnson walked into the hotel bedroom and stopped short. Beside Jenny on the bed, a man was struggling up with a sheepish look on his face. The free and easy days of liberated sex had not yet reached as far north as Tommel Castle. Couples sharing rooms were expected to be married, or at least to have the decency to

98

pretend to be.

'When you are ready, Miss Trask,' he said severely, 'I would like to see you in my office.'

He turned and walked out, slamming the door behind him.

'You'd better go,' said Jenny.

'Aw, come on, darlin',' said Brian, 'you're not afraid of that old toffee-nose.'

'No, no, you must go,' said Jenny almost hysterically. He got up and stretched lazily and put his clothes on while Jenny snatched up her own clothes and fled into the bathroom, her face red with shame. Once dressed, she stood there for a long time, hoping Brian would leave.

At last she opened the door. He was sitting on the bed and stood up when he saw her.

'Get out,' she said in a thin voice.

He grinned at her and winked.

She walked to the bedroom door and held it open. He gave her a slap on the bottom and then strolled out, whistling jauntily.

Jenny sank down into a chair. Her mouth felt dry and her head ached. How could she have done such a thing and with such a lout? How was it he had seemed so attractive, so interesting?

To him, she had been an easy lay, a pick-up, and now she had to face the manager.

But she didn't move. She just sat there, staring into space, and wishing, like Peta, she, too, could run away.

Hamish changed into dry clothes and went to the Fergusons' home to interview the two boys. Their father owned the Lochdubh Bakery and the family lived in a flat over the shop. He met Dr Brodie on the stairs. 'I've just given the children tranquillizers, Hamish,' said the doctor. 'Actually, I gave them a couple of indigestion tablets, but the parents think they're tranquillizers and that's all that matters. The trouble with people is they always expect some drug.'

Hamish went up and knocked at the door, which was opened by Mrs Ferguson, a thin waif of a woman except for her hands, which were large and strong and red.

'Och, Hamish,' she said when she saw him. 'Do you haff to speak to the weans now?'

'Only take a minute,' said Hamish. 'Where are they?'

'Watchin' the telly.'

Hamish went into the small cluttered living-room. The boys were in their dressing-gowns and pyjamas, watching a showing of 'Murder on Elm Street' on television. Hamish switched the set off. 'That'll not do you any good, boys.'

'We've had the pills,' said Jamie proudly. 'Dr Brodie said they wass anti-fright pills.'

'Nonetheless, you don't want to have nightmares when the effect wears off,' said Hamish. 'Read a comic instead.' He picked one

100

up from a pile on the sofa beside them. On the lurid cover a woman with her dress half off was about to be raped by a green alien. It was called *Revenge of Zork*. He put it down with a shudder. 'Maybe not. Now, boys'—he took out his notebook—'tell me how you found the body. Jamie, you'd better do it.'

'We wass up in the hills for a walk,' said Jamie, 'and Bill and me wanted tae look at the auld quarry. Then we saw her. She was awful. Great staring eyes.' He gulped.

'What time was this?'

Jamie looked bewildered. Bill piped up. 'It wass two. I've got my new watch.' He proudly held up a thin bird-like wrist to exhibit a cheap digital watch.

'Did you touch her?'

'No, we chust ran and ran as fast as we could.'

'Why did she ... did herself haff an apple in her mouth?' whispered Jamie.

Because someone probably jammed it in there, thought Hamish, but he closed his notebook and said instead, 'That's all for now, boys. If I think of anything else, I'll let you know.'

Frank Ferguson, the baker, was coming up the stairs as Hamish was leaving.

'Bad business,' he said. 'How are the bairns?'

'They'll be all right,' said Hamish, 'but stop them watching horror movies. They shouldn't be watching them at all.'

101

'Och, what can you do these days? They all watch them. Was it the fat wumman?'

'Yes, it was.'

'Ate herself to death?'

'Maybe,' said Hamish curtly. 'I'll let you know.'

102

CHAPTER FIVE

'She's the sort of woman now,' said
Mould ... 'one would almost feel
disposed to bury for nothing: and do it
neatly, too!'
—CHARLES DICKENS

The police cars drove up to the castle. The news of Peta's death spread like wildfire. Jenny still sat where she was, hugging herself, hearing the commotion and thinking in a dreary neurotic way that it was all to do with her shame.

And yet what had she done that was so terribly wrong? Admittedly it had happened to her before after too many drinks at an office party, when she had somehow ended up in bed with a solicitor's clerk. But that had been London, where morals were looser. And yet how could she, the romantic, the dreamer of knights on white chargers, have so easily leaped into bed with some labourer? Oh, the snobbery of sex. Something at the back of her mind was telling her wryly that had it been some successful businessman, she would not be feeling so low. Her friends had one-night stands and giggled about them. Perhaps she was a bit of a prude.

She rose shakily and went to the window of her room, which overlooked the front of the castle, and then drew back with a little cry of fright. There were police cars down there.

Scottish law was vastly different from English law. Could they have her arrested for immorality? A hammering at the door made her jump.

'Who's there?' she croaked.

'It's Maria. You'd better come downstairs.'

Sensible tweedy Maria, thought Jenny. She would look after her. Besides, Jenny was one of Maria's clients, so it was Maria's *duty* to look after her.

She opened the door.

'Peta's been found dead,' said Maria abruptly. 'The police want to interview everyone.'

All Jenny felt in that moment was a mixture of amazement and sheer gratitude. What was her lapse from grace compared to this?

'I'll come right away,' she said. 'What happened to Peta? Did she have an accident?'

'It appears not,' said Maria, running a worried hand through her short hair. 'They say it's murder.'

'How? When?'

'I'll tell you downstairs. I've got to get the others.'

Jenny walked down the stairs with a feeling of excitement. Peta murdered! Mr Johnson would have his hands too full with that to worry about her.

At reception she was told to go to the lounge,

104

where the rest of Checkmate were gathered, the police deciding to start with them and get around to the rest of the hotel guests later. Interviewing was to take place in the library.

* * *

Hamish Macbeth arrived in time for the first of the interviews. Blair glared at him, but Hamish quietly placed himself in a corner of the library.

Jessica Fitt was ushered in. She was, thought Hamish, only about thirty-two, but her prematurely grey hair made her look older. She had chosen clothes, consciously or unconsciously, which aged her as well. She had a vague, kind face, a thin mouth, and rather good eyes. She scratched one hip ferociously before she sat down and, once seated, proceeded to scratch her armpits in a nervous frenzy like some overwrought genteel monkey.

'Now, Miss Fitt,' said Blair in the Anglified accent he used for interviewing 'the nobs,' as he called them. 'Just a few questions. Mrs Worth has given us your file, so we know your background and address in London. What we want from you to begin with is your movements yesterday evening.'

'Let me see,' said Jessica, 'we all had dinner and Peta was there and then after dinner she went straight up to bed, so you must want to know about after that. Well, I sat in the lounge talking to Mr Trumpington and then he said there was a good movie on television and so we went to the television lounge to watch it.'

'You have television sets in your rooms, don't you?'

'Yes, but we are just friends and it would not be very correct to have a man in my room or go to his when there is a perfectly good television set downstairs.'

'What was the movie?'

'It was *Monsieur Hulot's Holiday*, Channel Four.'

'So what time would that be?'

'The movie started at nine-thirty. I don't know when it finished, but it isn't all that long, although you have to account for time for the ads.'

'We can check it in the newspaper,' said Blair. 'And then what did you do?'

'I went up to my room and went to bed. Maria has been organizing very early starts.'

'And Mr Trumpington?'

'I think he went to bed as well,' said Jessica and scratched her knee.

'Now, Miss Fitt, can you think of anyone in the party who would want to murder Peta Gore?'

'Oh, we all thought of killing her,' said Jessica and then wriggled miserably. 'Well, you know what I mean. "I could kill that woman," that kind of thing. But I cannot think of anyone who would actually have done it.'

'Do you know if Peta Gore was a wealthy

106

woman?'

'I know that. She was very wealthy. Worth three million.'

Blair's gaze sharpened. 'And how do you know that?'

'Because she told us. She had a fax from her accountant delivered to her at the table and she announced it. Someone said something about being surprised that marital agencies could rake in that sort of money and Peta said that it was due to her late husband's fortune and a good stockbroker.'

'That will be all for now, Miss Fitt.'

Jessica blinked at him in surprised relief and exited, scratching.

Blair looked round triumphantly. 'Well, we don't need tae look any further. She was worth three million, she doesn't have children, her niece is here with her, so the niece did it.'

'I don't think it's going to be as easy as that,' volunteered Hamish.

Blair gave a snort of disgust and demanded that Crystal be shown in.

Crystal had found something black to wear, although black was the only thing decent about her outfit. It consisted of a short divided skirt and a halter-top that left an expanse of bare, lightly tanned midriff. She sat down and crossed her legs.

'Your name is Crystal Debenham, and you are how old?' began Blair.

'Nineteen.'

'Job?'

'Not yet,' said Crystal huskily.

'What were your relations with your aunt?'

'Used to be all right,' said Crystal laconically. 'When I was at school, she'd come and take me out for tea and things like that. More than my parents did. She was jolly and good company.'

'And when did she ask you to come up here?'

'The morning she went. She'd found out Maria was up here with a group and phoned and asked me to come. So I packed and came. First time I'd seen Auntie since I got back from finishing school in Switzerland.'

'Do you benefit from your aunt's will?'

'Yes, I think I get all of it,' said Crystal equably.

'Therefore'—Blair hunched over the desk—'you had a strong motive for wanting rid of her.'

'Well, I wouldn't have liked her to leave the money to the old cat's home or something,' said Crystal, 'but Mummy and Daddy are quite rich, so it's not as if I was lusting after her millions, now was it?'

Blair gave her a look of irritation. 'What were you doing yesterday evening after dinner?'

She frowned in concentration. 'Oh, I know—I went upstairs same time as Auntie, went to my room. That's it.'

'What did you do in your room?'

108

'I painted my toe-nails.' Crystal opened her eyes to their fullest. 'That took simply ages because I'd painted them pink and then I thought, I've this new orange lipstick, why not paint them orange? So I took off the pink and put on the orange, and then of course I had to do my finger-nails.' She waggled long orange-painted finger-nails at him.

'And you did not see your aunt or hear her go out?'

'No, heard nothing. Can I go now?'

'Miss Debenham,' said Blair, his voice harsh and his accent slipping, 'yer Auntie was murdered and you don't seem to give a damn.'

'Maybe I'm in shock,' said Crystal, unmoved. 'But she had become a bit of a pain, slobbering all over her food. Gross!'

'Are there any witnesses who can testify that you were in your room all the time?'

'No, although I had the television on. Someone might have heard that.'

'You could have left that on while you lured your aunt out onto the moors into the quarry and murdered her,' roared Blair.

Crystal leaned back in her chair, and her voice was silky, 'Oh, do be so very careful, whatever your name is, before you start accusing me, or it will be me who puts you in the dock.'

Hamish leaned forward and surveyed her with interest. For under that sluttish appearance of hers, Crystal had all the tough

109

arrogance of a privileged background. She was either too stupid to cover up the fact that she expected to inherit her aunt's money and was not grieving over her death, or she was clever enough to tell the whole truth and nothing but the truth.

Blair looked like a baffled bull. 'We will be questioning you again, Miss Debenham, as soon as we have the forensic reports.'

'Do that,' said Crystal languidly and rose and swayed from the room.

Blair struck the desk with his fist. 'That bitch did it. I'll stake ma life on it.'

Jenkins, the maître d'hôtel, came in. Blair looked up angrily. 'We dinnae need you yet.'

'But I have vital information,' said Jenkins pompously.

'Out wi' it then!'

'I was passing Mrs Gore's bedroom earlier in the week and I heard Miss Maria Worth threatening her.'

'Ho, and whit did she say?'

'She shouted something like, "If I have to kill you to get rid of you, then I'll do it." It appears to be a well-known fact that Miss Worth wished to buy Mrs Gore out and Mrs Gore would not be bought out.'

'Thanks, Jenkins. Tell Maria Worth to step in here.'

'*Mr* Jenkins to you,' snapped the maître d'hôtel and stalked out.

'Still think Crystal did it?' asked Jimmy

110

Anderson.

'Aye, maybe. Let's see this wumman.'

Maria came in. It was evident to all she had been crying.

'Mrs Worth,' said Blair. 'I'll come straight to the point. You were overheard threatening to kill Peta Gore because she would not let you buy her out.'

'Yes, I did,' said Maria shakily. 'She was ruining everything with her appalling eating habits and by trying to flirt with the men. I was furious with her. But I did not kill her. It's just something one says when one is furious.'

'Oh, does one,' sneered Blair. 'Where were you last night?'

'I was in my room making calls to various clients in London to see how they were getting on. That would be right up until eleven o'clock. The hotel switchboard will have a record of those calls.'

'Mrs Gore could have been killed after eleven o'clock.'

'Well, I didn't do it,' said Maria wearily.

'Apart from her niece,' asked Hamish suddenly, 'did any of the clients of Checkmate know Peta before this trip to the Highlands?'

'I don't think so. Why?'

'I just wondered. I mean, you go into the background of your clients pretty thoroughly, do you not? Would there have been something there that Peta might have got hold of and threatened to use?'

111

'Peta took no interest in the business.'

Hamish remembered what Priscilla had told him. 'She had enough interest to operate your computer files and find out where you were,' he put in. 'I had this idea she might have had hopes of finding a husband for herself, which might lead her to check up on backgrounds.'

'Yes, she could have done that,' said Maria slowly. 'She never helped in the office, but she was very nosy, and yes, she did want another husband.'

'And did any of the men show any particular interest in her at any time?' Hamish asked.

'Ah'll ask the questions,' muttered Blair, his Glasgow accent getting thicker the more irritated he became. It was just like Hamish Macbeth to start cluttering up the scene with red herrings when it was clear that the only person with a real motive was Crystal.

But Maria was still looking at Hamish. 'Yes, three of them: John Taylor, Matthew Cowper, and Sir Bernard. It was after she had announced she was worth three million. I think those three got temporarily greedy. We were off to the theatre in Strathbane and they did rather vie for her attention.'

'Was anyone else heard threatening her life, apart from yourself?' demanded Blair.

'Well, just in a joky way. When we went out on a fishing-boat trip, I remember Jessica Fitt and Peter Trumpington capping each other's ideas about ways to kill Peta.'

'And why would they do that?'

'Peta Gore had become a thoroughly repulsive woman,' said Maria tearfully. 'She used to be such fun, such a nice person. That's why I'm crying. I can't help remembering what she used to be like.'

When Maria had left, Hamish said, 'I should tell you that Sean Gallagher, the cook, says that a picnic hamper is missing from the kitchen. It was taken along with some food during the night. It is also my belief that Sean has done time in Glasgow for assaulting his wife.'

Blair sent for Sean, who came in cringing. 'I gather ye've got a record,' said Blair without his usual pugnacity, for Blair himself was from Glasgow and Glasgow was the Holy City and Sean was therefore a spiritual brother.

'Only a few months,' whined Sean. 'Ah'm telling ye, it's this wimmin's lib. I only knocked the missus about a bit and they put me in the poky.'

'We'll come tae that later. Now about the stuff that's missing frae the kitchen.'

'Aye.' Sean looked relieved the subject had moved from his background. 'A picnic hamper, bread and ham, a meat-pie, fruit, a bottle o' Beaujolais—that's about as far as I can tell ye at the moment.'

'Would ye know if anyone had been in the kitchens during the night?'

'Not after ten o'clock.'

113

'What if someone wanted a late coffee?'

'There's a coffee-machine in the bar.'

'Aren't the kitchens locked at night?'

'No.'

Hamish shifted uneasily. Archie had told him about Sean's threatening Peta. But if he told Blair that, then the whole story about the cat would come out and Priscilla's business might collapse. He bit his lip and decided to interrogate Sean on his own later.

Blair asked Sean some more questions about whether he had seen any of the guests near Peta on the evening of her death and then let him go.

'Well, ah'm packing this in fur the night,' said Blair. 'We'll be back in the morning. We should hae a report from the pathologist by then and the forensic boys might hae matched these tyre tracks to one o' the cars here.'

The rest who were waiting in the hotel lounge were not relieved to be told they would be questioned in the morning. All had been geared up to getting it over with as soon as possible.

Jenny had gathered from Jessica that the police were interested in where everyone had been the evening before and heaved a sigh of relief. She did not want to discuss Brian Mulligan or have to produce him as a witness.

But her fears rushed back as Mr Johnson came up to her. 'Miss Trask,' he said severely, 'you took out the Volvo and left it standing in the storm with the sun-roof open and the windows. It took two maids an hour to clean and dry the inside of the car. Practically every other hotel would charge you for the use of a car. You abused the privilege and I am very angry with you.'

Jenny smiled at him. She was so relieved to find he was only angry about the car and not about her bedfellow.

'I am so sorry,' she said. 'Give me a bill for the maids' work and I will gladly pay it and for any damage to the car. I insist.'

'Well, I'm sure that won't be necessary,' said Mr Johnson, mollified. 'Just be more careful in future.'

He turned and addressed the whole group. 'I am afraid the press will be here in the morning. They are already phoning. We will have gamekeepers at the castle gates to keep them out, so you should not be disturbed. If any of them sneak in, report them to me.'

Jenny brightened. She wondered what to wear when she took a stroll down to the castle gates in the morning. She could already see her picture on the front page of the tabloids. Then her face fell. Of course she could not let that happen. Imagine all her friends knowing she was reduced to going to a marital agency to find a partner.

'Newspapers,' echoed Peter Trumpington in a hollow voice. He turned to Jessica. 'They'll ferret out everything about our backgrounds.'

Someone let out a hiss of dismay. Jessica

glanced quickly around but could not see anyone looking exceptionally disturbed. 'Why should you worry?' Jessica asked him. 'Do you have anything sordid in your past?'

'I was engaged to a starlet once and was in the papers a lot. She dumped me and that was in the papers. I don't want to be reminded of that humiliation.'

'Perhaps the best thing would be to make sure you don't speak to the press and then don't read any newspapers until this is all over.'

Peter looked at her with affection. 'You always say the right thing,' he said.

*   *   *

Sir Bernard found he was going 'off' Deborah. She made him feel ancient. She was wildly excited about the murder and fancied herself as some sort of Miss Marple, suspecting everyone in turn.

'Gosh,' she said, not without a touch of malice, 'look at the way you yourself were after her for her money. You could have got her to change her will and then bumped her off. Not that I can see you shoving an apple in her mouth. I would think a good clobber with a blunt instrument would be more in your line.'

'Shut up, you silly cow,' raged Sir Bernard and strode off.

Ever the professional despite her distress,

Maria made a mental note that she would need to pay the hotel bills for Deborah and Sir Bernard, for they certainly weren't going to make a match of it.

Nor did it look as if Mary French and Matthew Cowper were going to be much of a success either, for Mary said, 'I always think murders are done by very common people from places like Birmingham or Liverpool,' and Matthew, who was from Birmingham originally, said nastily, 'I should think someone like you would murder someone without thinking twice about it. It's all that schoolteaching. Gives people a power complex.' And Mary bridled and edged away from him.

John Taylor was reading a newspaper. He looked much older and his thin hands, freckled with liver spots, trembled as he held the paper. He was beginning to think the whole idea of Checkmate had been brought on by a brainstorm. He longed to see his son and daughter again, whatever they thought of him. He no longer wanted to marry anyone, he had never really wanted to marry anyone, only he had been so hurt and so vengeful. He felt as he had done all those years ago at his first day at boarding-school, when he had felt lost and alone and surrounded by threatening strangers.

He went into the bar for a drink, but that local policeman was sitting in a corner with

Priscilla and he didn't want to be anywhere near policemen until he had to face that interview. He felt that the police should really not dare interview such an eminent lawyer as himself.

*   *   *

'Take me through it from the beginning, Priscilla,' Hamish was saying. 'Start where you first met this lot and go on.'

So Priscilla told him about the unexpected arrival of Peta and her niece, the dreadful dinner, and then, after Peta had retired to her room, how Maria had told everyone that she had tried to buy Peta out but Peta wouldn't be bought and how she had offered to pay the hotel bill for any client who was not hitched by the end of the week.

'She can't expect any one of them to get hitched on such short acquaintance,' protested Hamish.

'I think she really meant if they had not found anyone whom they wanted to meet again after this visit. That's really the way it works. Follow-up visits are usually organized through the agency as well, because the agency can always step in and break off a relationship if one of the parties wants it terminated.'

'And how do you know so much about it?' asked Hamish suspiciously.

'I've got a friend in London who did the

118

round of the agencies. Actually, she found herself a very suitable husband. Wait a minute, there's something else ... something very important. I have it! I was serving coffee in the lounge and John Taylor said that someone in the group reminded him of someone he had seen once in court.'

'Did he say who?'

'No, he couldn't remember.'

'Need to check that out. Perhaps ma cousin in London, the one on the newspapers, can dig something up because Blair is going to pass on as little information to me as he can. Go on.'

'There's not much else that you don't know yourself. Except they were pairing off satisfactorily, that is, Matthew Cowper with Mary French, Deborah Freemantle with Sir Bernard, and Peter Trumpington with Jessica Fitt, up till they made that visit to the theatre. Everyone came back a bit edgy and cross. I noticed that. Everyone seemed to have gone off everyone, or perhaps it was just Sir Bernard and Deborah and Matthew and Mary.'

'I think I know the reason for that,' said Hamish and told her about Peta's millions.

'Oh, dear, then it must be Crystal. She's the only one who stood to gain anything out of this.'

'Perhaps. What do you make of her?'

'Crystal? Well, there doesn't seem to be much to understand. Beautiful in an over-made-up way. Doesn't dress like a lady, if that's not too old-fashioned a comment, but more like Eurotrash, the kind who go to wild parties in Paris before they all move on to the south of France, and who end up marrying an ugly millionaire, not for his money, but for his power. The Crystals of this world like autocrats. Would she kill her aunt? I don't see why. I can tell you, those skimpy tarty clothes of hers cost a small fortune, so her family must be well off.'

'I'll need to check up on Sean,' sighed Hamish. 'I covered up about the cat, but he was heard threatening her, for Archie told me. I'll try to keep that incident quiet, but if Sean did it or even proves to have a bad criminal record, I'll need to tell Blair. Why on earth didn't Johnson check him out?'

'Sean arrived just as that last chef we had walked out. Mr Johnson started him in the kitchen right away on trial and he cooked like a dream, so Mr Johnson was not going to question this gift from the gods at the beginning of the busy season.'

'Keep your ear to the ground,' said Hamish, 'and tell me if you can find anything out. That girl, Jenny, told me she felt there was someone mad in the group. She said she sensed it.'

'And when did she say this?'

'She came down to the police station earlier this week.'

'When will you ever learn, Hamish! The little drip made that up to get your attention.'

120

'Flattering of you to say so, but there might be something in it. Well, I'd best be off and phone my cousin.'

When Hamish walked outside, a forensic team were supervising the loading of the hotel's Volvo onto a truck. 'That was quick,' said Hamish to one of them. 'You matched the tyre tracks.'

'Aye,' said the man he had spoken to, 'but a fat lot of good it'll do us. The car was left out in thon storm with the sun-roof and the windows all open and the manager here tells me it was soaked and so he got a couple of maids to clean it out thoroughly. I doubt if we'll get anything from it now.'

'Could it have been left out deliberately?'

'Could hae been. But it was some silly wee lassie, so Johnson says.'

Hamish watched until the car on the back of the truck moved off and went to the police Land Rover. Jenny Trask was sitting in the passenger seat, her face white in the gloom.

'What do you want?' asked Hamish crossly. It had been a long day and he was anxious to get home.

'Why have they taken that car away?' asked Jenny.

'Because that was the car that Peta or her murderer drove up to the quarry.'

'Oh, God.' Jenny put her face in her hands and began to cry.

Hamish sat patiently until her sobs had

121

subsided and then said, 'You were the one that left it out in the rain?'

Jenny gulped and nodded.

'That's no great crime,' he said gently. 'Why and when did you take the car out?'

'It was late this morning,' said Jenny tremulously, 'I went down to the police station to look for you and you weren't there. So ... so I went into the bar and this man bought me a drink and we got talking. His name is Brian Mulligan.'

'Big Irish chap, works for the forestry?'

Jenny nodded. 'I'll be glad when that one moves on,' said Hamish. 'He's a devil with the women.'

'We drank a lot. He seemed so nice and friendly and so we went back to the hotel and had drinks in the bar and then ... and then ... I took him up to my room.'

'Aren't you the shy one,' said Hamish cynically.

'It wasn't me. It was the drink! And this weird place. I heard the storm but I forgot about the car. Mr Johnson came up to give me a row about the car and found me in bed with Brian and now he'll tell the police.'

'So? You're free and single. Johnson's a wee bit straitlaced, but don't let that worry you.'

'I feel so ashamed,' whispered Jenny. 'You must think I'm a slut.'

'No, of course I don't. Look, you told me the other night that you thought one of the party was mad. Did you mean that?'

'I did at the time,' said Jenny, 'but now I'm not so sure. It was the heat, you see, and then ... up here, you don't feel you're in Britain ... like being in a foreign country. I think ... I think that's why I went to bed with Brian. I felt so far away from London, so far away from the conventions.'

Hamish looked at her gloomily. He reflected that she was the kind of nice girl who nonetheless gave British girls such a poor name on the Continent. She belonged to the kind who travelled to, say, Greece, and ended up in bed with a hotel waiter the first night of arrival, liberated by drink and by being so far from home.

'Take my advice,' he said, 'and tell Blair about the car. You don't need to tell him about Mulligan. It's not as if you need an alibi for that time. I'll hae a wee word with Mr Johnson.'

'Oh, thank you, Hamish.' Jenny threw her arms about him and planted a wet kiss on his cheek.

Through the windscreen he could see the pale blur of a face at one of the castle windows looking down on them, a face with the shine of blonde hair above. Priscilla!

'Off you go,' he said severely, leaning across her and opening the passenger door.

He drove down to Lochdubh, feeling cross. Why should he care whether Priscilla saw him or not?

He completed his chores and then phoned his cousin, Rory Grant, who worked as a reporter on a London newspaper.

'Hamish! Do you have to call in the middle of the night?' groaned Rory.

'I'm sorry to wake you up,' began Hamish.

'You didn't wake me up. I've just come in after taking one of my colleagues to the funny farm. It's amazing how people can go stark-raving bonkers in a newspaper and no one notices until they start to eat the carpet or something. That's the trouble about jobs that encourage eccentrics. So what's happened? Another murder?'

'Aye, and I've some names here for you to check. You do that for me and I'll give your rag first bite of the cherry when we get the murderer.' He briefly outlined the case and gave Rory a list of the suspects.

After he had put the phone down, he prepared himself for bed, turning over the case in his mind. Would it take someone powerful to hold Peta down and jam an apple in her mouth? Not necessarily. She was such a huge woman that she would flounder like a beached whale.

Rain pattered against the bedroom window and the wind howled down the loch outside. The halcyon days of summer were over, although it was still August. Winter came early in the far north.

He cursed Peta in his heart for having brought death to his village. If ever a woman had been begging to be murdered, that woman was Peta Gore!

CHAPTER SIX

Down to Gehenna or up to the Throne,
He travels the fastest who travels alone.
                              —RUDYARD KIPLING

Another day dawned wet and windy. The members of Checkmate were turned out of their rooms, which had already been searched but which were to be searched again. The type-written note supposed to have come from Peta had not been typed on any machine at the hotel. But Crystal volunteered that her aunt had had a portable typewriter which was missing, along with Peta's luggage.

The day's questioning began with Deborah Freemantle. Blair thought she was a jolly and friendly type and not at all stuck up like any of the others, that was, until she eagerly told him that she read a lot of detective stories and would like to help him solve the case.

Biting down on his bad temper, Blair said heavily, 'There isnae a detective story on the market which bears any relation tae real life.'

'Oh, really,' said Deborah brightly, 'you don't look like the sort of man who reads anything.' She had not meant to be bitchy, it was meant as a straightforward observation, but she plunged even lower in Blair's opinion.

Nevertheless, he took her through her

movements on the evening Peta had died with a certain amount of civility. Blair saved the worst of his bullying for the lower classes. 'I went out for a walk,' said Deborah. 'I went over to the stables to see if they had any horses, but they didn't have any. I met one of the gamekeepers, and he said Priscilla used to have a horse but it died some time ago and that the colonel was thinking of turning the stables into guest-rooms.'

'Do you know the gamekeeper's name?'

'No, but he was small with close-set eyes and red hair. He was wearing...' Deborah was just getting into her lady-detective act when Hamish interrupted. 'That'd be Dougie.'

'Aye, we'll see him later. Now what can you tell us about the others, Miss Freemantle?'

'Gosh! That's a tall order. Crystal's an empty-headed type and I don't think she thinks of much other than clothes. I don't think she particularly disliked her aunt. Mary French terrifies me.'

Blair looked at her alertly. 'Why?'

Deborah giggled. 'She's just like my old form mistress. A real terror.'

Blair frowned. 'Go on. John Taylor.'

'Dry old stick. Bit of a bore. Prissy. Couldn't murder a fly.'

'Jessica Fitt?'

'Oh, her. Dreary.' Deborah leaned forward. 'It's my opinion that Peter Trumpington has an Oedipus complex.'

127

'Whit's that, in the name?'

'A man who loves his mother or women who remind him of his mother,' said Deborah loftily.

'Spare me the psychology,' groaned Blair. 'Maria Worth?'

'Oh, she's nice. I mean, what you see is what you get. She wanted rid of Peta, but she wouldn't kill her.'

'Sir Bernard Grant?'

Hamish saw Deborah's normally cheerful face harden. 'One of those ruthless business types. He could have paid someone to bump her off.'

'Why?'

'Because that's what that kind of man does!'

'Miss Freemantle,' said Hamish, 'on the day of the boat trip you were holding hands with Sir Bernard. Why the change of heart?'

Deborah blushed, an ugly blotchy-red blush. 'He was begging me to marry him, but of course Mummy and Daddy would not be pleased. He's too old and a bit common.'

'Isn't your change of heart because Sir Bernard was pursuing Peta the minute he learned she was worth three million and you felt your nose had been put out of joint?' pursued Hamish.

'Well, really, what an insane idea!' spluttered Deborah. 'You should leave the questioning to your superiors. You do not

128

have the experience for a murder inquiry.'

Blair gave her a more tolerant look. 'Aye, well, we'll be talking to you again later. Send Mr Taylor in.'

'Before you talk to Mr Taylor,' said Hamish quickly, 'at the beginning of his visit, he said something about having seen one of the party before, and in court, too, but he could not remember which one.'

'We should know which one for ourselves soon,' said Blair, trying to look uninterested. 'The backgrounds on this lot should be coming over the fax soon.'

John Taylor came in and sat down quietly. 'I believe,' said Blair, 'that you said earlier that you knew one of the party had been in court. Can you tell us which one?'

'No,' said John. 'It was just an impression. I have attended so many cases. Probably wrong.'

His legs were crossed and his hands were clasped on one knee. Hamish noticed them tighten as he said this and wondered whether he really had recognized the person. Blair asked him about his movements on the night of Peta's death and John said he had gone to bed. He was feeling his years.

'I have to ask you this, sir,' said Blair in a grovelling voice because lawyers terrified him, particularly top-ranking English ones, 'why does a gentleman like yourself employ the services of Checkmate?'

129

'That is simple,' said John. 'I am getting on in years. My children left home long ago and are now married with families of their own. I am lonely. I am too old to start dating and it is hard for me to find the right kind of female.'

'Whom had Maria chosen for you?' interposed Hamish quickly.

'That schoolteacher, Mary French. Most unsuitable.'

'She certainly is considerably younger than you,' said Hamish.

'That kind of woman was born looking old,' said John drily.

'But,' protested Hamish, who had sneaked a look at Maria's files before the questioning began, 'you said you wanted a woman of child-bearing years. Why?'

'Such information,' said John angrily, 'is confidential, and Checkmate undertook never to reveal any of it.'

'They weren't expecting a murder case,' said Hamish patiently. 'Why?'

John Taylor took a deep breath. Oh, what had ever persuaded him to become a client of Checkmate!

'I am not going to tell you,' he said in measured tones, 'because it has no bearing on the case. The information in my file must be kept secret from the press, otherwise I will sue Checkmate, and you, too, for breaking confidentiality. Do I make myself clear?'

He had risen to his feet as he said this and

130

looked formidable.

'Now, now,' said Blair in a wheedling tone, 'you mustn't pay any attention to our local bobby, sir. That'll be all for now.'

When John Taylor had walked out, Blair rounded on Hamish.

'That's a Queen's Counsel, you daft pillock. Ye cannae go around asking cheeky questions.'

'The job of a good policeman,' said Hamish primly, 'is to ask cheeky questions. He was lying.'

'Havers. Send the next one in, Anderson.'

Peter Trumpington was next. He said that, yes, he had watched a French movie with Jessica. The only reason he could think that someone might have killed Peta was because of sheer disgust. 'You didn't see her,' he said to Blair. 'Mealtimes were a nightmare.'

Sir Bernard was next. He said he had gone out for a walk. He was asked whether he had been paying court to Peta and he said frankly it had crossed his mind to try his luck because three million pounds was not to be sneezed at.

'And was that why Miss Freemantle became angry with you?' asked Hamish.

'I suppose so,' said Sir Bernard miserably. 'Such a silly little girl.'

'A silly little girl you were holding hands with on the day of the boat trip,' put in Hamish.

'Well, I thought she was a jolly sort, but then

131

I went off her,' said Sir Bernard. 'Anyway, what has all this got to do with the murder?'

'We're just feeling our way, sir,' said Blair, throwing a nasty look at Hamish, a look tinged with jealousy. Hamish's Highland lack of snobbery and his ability to ask questions of rich and poor without making any difference between them always riled Blair.

Matthew Cowper, Jenny, and Mary French were still to be interviewed. Sir Bernard came out but said nothing to them and disappeared into the grounds. They all waited anxiously to be called.

But inside, Blair had just received a phone call from Peta Gore's lawyers. 'Now here's something,' he said, his piggy eyes gleaming. 'On the evening of her death, Peta phoned up her lawyer at home, that's the senior partner, Mr Wotherspoon, and told him she would be changing her will. He said naturally that she should wait until her return to London and call in at the office and sign the papers, but she said she wanted it done right away and would fax him a temporary will in the morning. "That niece of mine is a useless slut," she said. But she didnae say who the new beneficiary was.

'Now if Crystal knew her aunt was about to change her will, there's a motive. Get her in here again!'

So Matthew and Mary and Jenny watched as Crystal was led back in for more questioning, all three wishing it were their turn so that they could get the ordeal over with.

Hamish slipped out of the interview room and went in search of John Taylor. He found him in his room, sitting in an armchair by the window reading the newspapers.

'What is it now?' asked John wearily.

'I just wanted to make sure you didn't really remember which one it was you once saw in court.'

'No, and now I don't think I really recognized anyone. There is a great deal of the theatre about us barristers and a desire to show off. Not very worthy motives.'

'I do not want to upset you,' said Hamish kindly, 'but I really would like to know why at your age you were thinking of starting a family again.'

The window was open and a line of pine trees outside bent in the rising wind. Clouds covered the mountain-tops. A bleak and alien landscape, thought John. Here no bird sings. He longed to be home again. He thought Hamish looked a decent-enough fellow, but he had no intention of telling him the truth.

'You are a young man,' he said. 'I am old and no longer feel immortal. I have a craving for a family life again. My wife died when the children were young and I brought them up. It was sometimes tiresome and sometimes arduous, but always rewarding.' He suddenly remembered little bright images, Brian scoring a century at cricket for his school, Penelope

133

going off to her first dance. To his horror, his eyes filled with tears and he brushed them angrily away.

'I am sorry to have disturbed you,' said Hamish awkwardly. He went downstairs and back to the library just as Jenny Trask was being brought in for questioning. Crystal had obviously survived the second bout of interrogation.

Jenny sat down facing Blair, disliking his heavy features, his truculent look. She looked around for Hamish, but he was sitting behind her.

'Now, Miss Trask,' said Blair, 'you have caused us a great deal of trouble. Whit ... what possessed ye to leave all the windows and the sun-roof open in that Volvo?'

'It was hot when I drove back,' said Jenny, 'and I forgot about it. I was tired. I went to bed.'

'The barman said you had drinks in the bar wi' one o' the forestry workers. Old friend?'

'No, I had only met him that day ... in Lochdubh.'

'Oh, a pick-up,' sneered Blair, and Jenny winced.

Please God, she thought, don't let the barman have seen us both going upstairs. But he had been off somewhere. The place looked empty.

'Right, Miss Trask. Now tell us what you were doing on the evening Mrs Gore was

134

murdered?'

'Oh, that. I took one of the hotel cars and drove...'

'You what!'

'Oh.' Jenny put her hand to her mouth and paled. 'It was the Volvo, but I went to the police station, didn't I, Hamish?'

'And what were you seeing this Romeo of the Heilands about ... or shouldn't I ask?' demanded Blair.

'I was only going to tell him that I felt uneasy, that I thought there was someone mad in the castle. Didn't I, Hamish?'

'Yes,' agreed Hamish, 'but you told me later that you thought you were mistaken. Miss Trask only stayed about fifteen minutes,' he said to Blair. 'She must have left about nine-thirty.'

'And did you go straight back to the castle?' asked Blair.

'Yes.'

'Did anyone see you?'

'Yes, the barman. I went straight to the bar for a coffee.'

'We'll check that. See here, Miss Trask, I don't like coincidences, and you had that car out twice and you left it so that any clues would be destroyed.'

'You mean that was the car used by the murderer?' whispered Jenny.

What is she playing at? thought Hamish crossly. She knows very well it was that car.

135

'Yes, and if that murderer was you, I would advise you to confess and get it over with,' shouted Blair suddenly.

Jenny burst into tears and Blair gave a sound of disgust and ordered Macnab to take her out.

'Who's next in this poxy lot?' growled Blair, consulting his list. 'Let's see. Matthew Cowper. Send him in.'

But at that moment, the phone beside Blair rang. He picked it up and listened intently. A slow, evil smile spread across his face. When he put the phone down, he looked triumphantly around. 'Ah've found the killer,' he said, his Glaswegian accent at its broadest. No need to toady any more to the nobs. The great Blair had found the murderer.

'Oh, aye,' said Jimmy Anderson cynically. 'Who?'

'Mary French.'

'Aw, away wi' ye,' said Jimmy Macnab, startled into impertinent insubordination. 'Thon's naethin' more than a wee bittie o' a schoolteacher.'

'She's killed afore,' said Blair with a grin. 'That was the Yard. She was up in court for murder ten years ago. She killed her own mither.'

'Did she go to prison?' asked Hamish, startled.

'Naw, she got off. Said her mither was dying o' cancer and had begged her to give her an overdose of sleeping pills. And the jury

136

believed her. Mercy killing. Pah! They kill once, they'll kill again.'

'And was John Taylor prosecuting?'

Blair glared at Hamish. He had forgotten to ask. 'That disnae matter now. Get her in here and we'll charge her.'

'Wait a minute,' said Hamish. 'There is no proof!'

'Ah'll get proof, laddie. You mind yer place and get back to your polis station and check on yer sheep-dip papers and leave this tae the big yins.'

Mary French was led in. Blair began to caution her as Hamish Macbeth walked out.

He went in search of Priscilla and eventually found her outside, supervising the building of the new gift shop.

'What's the matter, Hamish?' she said when she saw his face.

'Blair's charging Mary French with the murder.'

'Why?'

'She killed her mother and got off with it. The woman was dying of cancer and the jury chose to believe it was a mercy killing. Blair's a fool. I've been ordered back to the police station.'

'Look, Hamish, there's really not much I can do here. Daddy phoned in a rage. Says he's not coming back till it's all over. I could come down to the police station with you.'

'Why?'

'Well, I've helped you to sort things out before. We could sit down and have a cup of tea and—'

'No, I'm far better off on my own,' snapped Hamish.

He marched off, cursing himself for having been so rude but yet unable to go back and apologize. Blair's stupidity had rattled him. Also, he remembered the days when he had been so yearningly in love with Priscilla and he did not want to put himself in any danger of those days returning.

Mary French was being led out to the police car. Her face was tight with strain, but she looked grim and composed. A little huddle of people at the door watched her go. Maria, John, Jenny, Matthew, Sir Bernard, Jessica and Deborah.

They watched in silence until the police car disappeared down the drive.

Deborah approached Hamish as he reached his Land Rover. 'I say,' she gasped, 'why are they taking Mary away?'

'I don't know,' said Hamish testily. 'I'm not on the case.'

'I mean, why would Mary kill Peta?'

'God knows,' said Hamish, unlocking the car door.

'You don't think she did it!' cried Deborah. 'You think they've made a terrible mistake.'

'Aye, maybe.'

'I say, gosh, this is exciting. Here's your

138

chance to make your mark. With my help, we could probably find out who did it.'

Another Watson, thought Hamish sourly, and the wrong one. 'Policing should be left to the police,' he said coldly. 'Don't interfere, Miss Freemantle.'

Deborah pouted and bounced off in a huff. She had hitherto led an uncomplicated life, without many ups or downs. But Sir Bernard's rejection of her had hurt. If only *she* could find the murderer. Now in a detective story she had read recently, the clever detective, Sir Bartholomew Styles, had caused the murderer to betray himself at his cousin's stately home by letting everyone there think he knew who the murderer was.

Then Deborah remembered a game she and the other girls had played in the sixth form at the expensive boarding-school she had attended. One of them would say to one of the girls in the fifth, 'I saw you. You shouldn't have done that. I think I'll have to tell someone.' If it didn't work on that girl, it was tried on another, but it usually worked, schoolgirls having often been up to some small sin they didn't want found out. Deborah and her friends would then award a prize of ten pounds at the end of the term to whichever one of them had 'scored' the highest.

Why not try it on this lot? thought Deborah, bouncing with excitement.

She started with Matthew Cowper. 'I saw

you, you know,' she whispered and then walked quickly away. Matthew stared after her, his hands clenched. He had stolen a bottle of old malt whisky out of the bar when no one was looking. He could easily have paid for it, but it had given him a kick to take it. Damn! What if she told that manager? He would tell the police. Matthew decided to borrow a car and go and see if he could buy a bottle of the same brand and replace it. That must have been what Deborah meant. She could not possibly mean anything else. She couldn't have *seen* anything else. Could she?

'I saw you,' said Deborah reproachfully to Jenny. 'But I haven't told the police yet.'

Jenny thought she meant the episode with Brian Mulligan and her face went white. 'You say one word,' she hissed, 'and I'll wring your neck.'

'I saw you do it,' said Deborah to Sean, the cook. He was chopping meat. He raised the cleaver, 'I'll shut yer mouth for ye, you stupitt bitch, and I'll take this cleaver through your heid.'

Deborah squeaked with fright and fled from the kitchen. But Sean's reaction had elated her. Deborah was young enough to feel immortal. Besides, she was convinced that the murderer would not now murder anyone else, but might, with her 'stirring up,' become rattled enough to betray himself—or herself.

140

'Isn't there something you should be telling the police?' said Deborah to Maria and had the satisfaction of seeing Maria start and flush guiltily. Next came Jessica. Her reaction, too, was satisfying, as was that of Peter Trumpington.

John Taylor said crossly, 'Saw what? Oh, never mind, run along.' That made Deborah pause, for he had made her feel like a silly schoolgirl, but she then saw Sir Bernard approaching and the temptation was too great. 'I know everything about you,' said Deborah, 'and gosh, am I glad I decided not to marry you. I know what you did.'

Sir Bernard's face turned dark with anger and he marched off without replying.

As Deborah watched him go, a pang of rejection pierced her again. Priscilla was working at the reception, sitting behind a computer making out bills, for the rest of the guests were free to go provided they left their addresses, and most had decided to leave.

'I saw you,' said Deborah.

Priscilla looked up.

'What?'

'I saw you.'

'Saw me doing what?'

'You know,' said Deborah mysteriously and walked away.

When they all sat down to dinner that night, the atmosphere was strained. It should have been relaxed, now that someone had been

141

arrested, but Deborah kept discussing the case, chewing over every little morsel, saying over and over again that she happened to *know* that Mary had not done it.

'You're just showing off,' said Sir Bernard.

Deborah glared at him and tossed her head. 'That's all you know,' she said defiantly.

After dinner, everyone seemed to be avoiding everyone else, with the exception of Peter Trumpington and Jessica Fitt, who appeared to have become inseparable.

They were all sitting around the lounge, but well away from each other, when John Taylor finally stood up. 'I'm going to bed,' he announced to no one in particular. He strode to the doorway and then paused, 'Good heavens! With someone arrested for the murder, that means we can all go home!'

They all brightened. Home! Outside, a chill wind was blowing and a log fire had been lit in the lounge. Home to buses and tubes and noise and streets, and crowds and crowds of people. Home to London, far away from this weird, twisted countryside of mountain, loch, and moorland where the old gods rode the wind.

'Don't go,' called Sir Bernard suddenly to John's retreating back. 'I'll order champagne for everybody.'

John came back and sat down. Sir Bernard pushed down an old-fashioned china bell-push on the wall and the barman came in to take the order for champagne. They all chattered and laughed. Matthew Cowper told some really dreadful jokes which everyone, inebriated with relief and champagne, enjoyed immensely.

Deborah began to feel ashamed of herself. If Mary had not done the murder, then some madman had come across Peta on the moors. Not one of these sane, regular people could attack anyone, let alone murder them.

She set herself to enjoy the impromptu champagne party and was one of the last to leave the lounge.

Only Jessica and Peter were left when she rose to go to bed.

'Aren't you tired?' Peter asked Jessica.

'A little,' she replied. 'But it's warm and bright and cosy here. I feel safe. But once I get to my room, all the fears come back.'

'Do you think Mary did it?'

'I don't know,' said Jessica slowly. 'But I can't help hoping so. It would be awful to think there was a murderer still amongst us.'

*   *   *

It was nearly midnight, but Priscilla decided to call on Hamish. She wondered why he had been so angry and if she had done or said anything to offend him. Then she was worried about Deborah. Priscilla had attended an English boarding-school and knew all about the 'I saw you' game. She was sure Deborah had tried it on the rest. In any case, she would

143

feel easier if she told Hamish about it.

Hamish heard the hotel Range Rover arrive. He recognized the sound of the engine. Priscilla. He was on the phone to Rory in London and taking down notes on the background of the members of Checkmate. He decided to stay where he was and not answer the door. He did not want to see Priscilla, did not want any more intimate midnight chats until he had got his feelings under control again. He ignored the banging at the kitchen door. Rory was saying, 'Yes, Mary French was found not guilty of the death of her mother, and yes, John Taylor was the prosecuting counsel. What else? Oh, there was some nasty rumours floating around that Sir Bernard Grant had been dealing in arms, but nothing really came of that. Peter Trumpington's been in the gossip columns, but nothing sinister. John Taylor once punched a policeman outside the Old Bailey for not showing him "due respect" when all the bobby had been trying to do was to stop him parking on a double-yellow line. But nothing odd about that. He's a great old character. Mary French hit the newspapers again when she made a speech to the pupils advocating the return of caning. But you don't think she did it.'

'I didnae say that.' Hamish heard the Range Rover drive off and felt suddenly bleak. 'What about Peta Gore herself?'

'Married to millionaire Bobby Gore, who

144

died in '82 and left her a fortune. A few society snippets, that's all.'

'And Maria?'

'Nothing on her background. Only a little piece on the society page of the *Express* saying that it was through Checkmate run by Maria Worth that Lord Bullsden met his bride.'

Hamish sighed. 'Nothing there to bite on. But how Blair thinks he can charge Mary French wi' the murder when he hasn't a shred of proof, I don't know.'

* * *

Deborah yawned and put down the detective story she had been reading and switched out her bedside light. Tomorrow she would start making plans to go home. But the minute the light was out, she felt awake and restless. She had made such a fool of herself. That editor in the office, Sally Blye, kept saying things like, 'Oh, why don't you grow up, Deborah? I swear to God you think you're still at school.' School had been super. One knew where one was at school. But none of her old school chums had remained the same. One minute, it seemed, they were regular jolly girls in school uniform, and the next, they were mature sirens in lipstick and the latest fashions. She wished the wind would stop howling. It was increasing in force, great buffets of it striking the tower room where she slept.

145

She was so preoccupied with her thoughts that she did not see the door of her bedroom open gently, did not see the dark figure creeping in. She was suddenly thinking how sunny and hopeful it had all been at the beginning of the week, how her marriage to Sir Bernard had seemed inevitable, and then, how at the smell of Peta's fortune, he had rushed off after her and of how cruel and rude he had subsequently become.

She was sleeping in a double bed. 'Damn,' she said and flung herself restlessly to the other side of the bed just as something heavy swept down with vicious force and struck the pillow where her head had been only a moment before. She could feel the wind of it. She rolled onto the floor and under the bed, screaming loudly as she went, huge, great rending screams. She heard footsteps hurrying out.

She crouched there, knees drawn up to her chin, screaming 'Help me, help me' over and over again.

Priscilla ran to the turret steps. She pressed the light switch at the bottom of the stairs but the light did not come on. In a blind panic, she ran straight up to Deborah's room and clawed at the switch by the door. 'Thank God,' she muttered as the room was flooded with bright electric light.

She knelt down beside the bed and shouted over the noise of Deborah's screaming, 'It's all right. It's me ... Priscilla. *It's all right!*'

Deborah slowly crawled out, babbling, 'Someone tried to kill me.'

Priscilla helped her to her feet and put an arm about her shoulders.

'It must have been a nightmare,' she said soothingly. 'It must—'

She broke off and stared at the bed. Deborah stared too and then began to scream again.

Feathers were floating in the draughty air of the tower room. And lying on the bed was a meat cleaver which had struck the pillow with such force that it had split it in half.

CHAPTER SEVEN

Sweet is revenge—especially to women.
                                    —LORD BYRON

Hamish answered the phone and listened in alarm as he heard of the attack on Deborah. 'And I know why it happened,' added Priscilla.

'Why?'

'I'll tell you when you get here, Hamish, but if you had not decided to play the Lone Ranger and had answered the door when I called this evening, we wouldn't be in this fix.'

When Hamish arrived at Tommel Castle, it was to find them all gathered in the lounge, along with the hotel servants and Mr Johnson, the manager, who greeted him with words to the effect that Sean had been locked in his room.

Hamish then listened to what had nearly happened to Deborah and phoned Strathbane and reported an attempted murder.

He went back to the lounge and his eyes fell on Priscilla. 'Before I see Sean, Priscilla,' he said, 'you'd best explain how it is you know why this attempt on Miss Freemantle's life took place.'

Priscilla explained about the 'saw you' game, adding that as Deborah had tried it out on her, she had no doubt tried it out on everyone else.

'Is that right?' Hamish asked Deborah. 'Were you playing a game?'

'You didn't think Mary had done it,' said Deborah tearfully, 'and so I thought I would help a bit. I mean, if someone else was guilty and I startled them, he or she might betray themselves ... or so I thought.'

'I won't waste time at the moment with lecturing you on playing a spiteful and dangerous game,' said Hamish. 'I know you've had a terrible shock. Dr Brodie will be here shortly to look after you and give you a sedative, but right now you are going to have to pull yourself together and tell me what reactions you got. Now, first, Sean, the cook.'

'It must have been him,' said Deborah through white lips.

'Why?'

'I said to him, "I saw you do it," and he raised his meat cleaver and said he would shut my mouth for me and I ran away.'

'And that wasn't enough to persuade you to drop it?' marvelled Hamish. 'Did you approach Maria Worth?'

'Yes, I said something like I knew there was something she should be telling the police and she looked awfully guilty.'

'Did you look guilty?' Hamish asked Maria.

'I suppose I did,' said Maria. 'There certainly is something I forgot to tell the police. Before Peta was discovered dead, I went to her

149

room to make sure she really had gone. Everything appeared to have been packed up except her sponge-bag, which was hanging from one of the taps in the bathroom. I took it and put it in my room and then forgot about it. I really did, until Deborah's question reminded me. I'll get it for you now.'

She went out. 'Next?' asked Hamish.

'Matthew Cowper, he looked terribly guilty,' said Deborah.

Matthew had his story ready. 'I'd gone down one night, looking for a drink,' he said. 'With all the fuss, they'd forgotten to put the grille down over the bar. I took a bottle of Scotch. I'd forgotten to tell Johnson or to replace it until Deborah played her silly trick on me and I thought that must be what she meant.'

'So you took the whole bottle of Scotch up to your room and drank the lot?'

'No, of course not. I'm not a drunk. There was plenty left in the morning.'

'And yet that didn't remind you to tell Johnson or the barman you had taken the bottle? Pay him now. If this wasn't a murder inquiry, I would seriously think of charging you with theft. Miss Freemantle, who else seemed guilty?'

Deborah was recovering from her fright and even beginning to enjoy being the centre of attention. 'Jenny, Miss Trask,' she said eagerly. 'She was in such a state, she threatened to wring my neck.'

150

'You know what I thought she meant,' cried Jenny. 'You know, Hamish.'

'And that's all it was?' asked Hamish, remembering the forestry worker.

'I swear.'

'Okay, next?'

Deborah said defiantly, 'Sir Bernard looked mad as anything.'

'Sir Bernard?'

'She said something about being glad she hadn't married me because of what I did. I thought she was bitching on about my interest in Peta. To be quite frank, I don't come out of that looking very good, but the thought of those millions got to me.'

'Mr Taylor?'

'I didn't know what she was talking about, so I told her not to be so silly.'

'Miss Fitt?'

'It was only after she had gone that I realized I had nothing to feel guilty about. But I'm one of those people who feel guilty about anything. Everything in the whole wide world is my fault,' said Jessica.

'And Mr Trumpington?'

'I thought she'd overheard me talking to Maria,' mumbled Peter.

'I'm afraid I must know what you said,' prompted Hamish.

'Why?' put in Jessica fiercely. 'If Jenny can keep her secret, so can Peter. Take him outside

151

and ask him there.'

'It's all right,' said Peter, taking her hand in his. 'The fact is, I told Maria I thought we'd make a pretty good pair. Stupid way to propose, isn't it?'

Jessica's grey face became suffused with colour and her eyes shone. It was her one moment of beauty. She clasped his hand tightly.

'The police from Strathbane will soon be here,' said Hamish. 'I will go and question the cook. Then I will return and take statements from you one after another, if they have not arrived by the time I'm through with the cook.'

Mr Johnson led him to the cook's bedroom and unlocked the door.

'I'll be all right,' said Hamish. 'Go and ask the staff if they saw anyone on the tower stair and if there is any sign of that missing light bulb. Priscilla said the light would not come on, so I suppose someone removed it.'

Sean was sitting crouched on the end of his bed. He was fully dressed.

'Now, Sean,' said Hamish severely, 'I'm not going to be able to keep quiet about that cat anymore. You threatened to kill Peta. You threatened to kill Deborah Freemantle and, lo and behold, someone takes your meat cleaver and does just that. I suppose it is your meat cleaver?'

'Aye, it's gone,' said Sean wearily. 'Johnson took me to look for it when ah got back frae the

152

village.'

Hamish's eyes sharpened. 'Back from the village?'

'I wus down fur a wee dram wi' Dougie, the gamekeeper.'

'Where?'

'The bar. There wus a lot in, so they kep' it open late.'

'When did you get back?'

'Dougie waud know. It was himself that ran me back. I came in the door and Johnson grabs me and drags me off to the kitchen yelling about the meat cleaver. It's gone, so he says ah've tae stay in my room till the polis comes.'

Hamish wondered why he should feel so relieved that this unlovely cook had an alibi. Probably for Priscilla's sake, he decided after a moment's reflection.

'As long as you've got witnesses to say you weren't in the castle, you should be all right.' Hamish looked down at him thoughtfully. 'How bad was the attack on your wife?'

'Oh, her, broke her jaw.'

'Why? Were you drunk, man?'

'Naw, ah fixed the Sunday dinner. Sole à l'Italienne, it wus.'

'And?'

'The silly cow looks at it and says, "Whaur's the ketchup?" So I let her have it.'

'Your last job, I remember from your file, was at the Glasgow Queen. Why did you leave?'

Sean stared at the floor.

'Out wi' it. I'll find out anyway.'

'The boss's missus—we called her auld tattie-heid—says ah was spending too much time ower the soups. Ah says they had to thicken and she says ah was tae thicken them up wi' cornflower. Sacrilege, that! I telt her she wus a greasy penny-pinching auld whore.'

'Oh, my. Look, Sean, when this is over, if it iss ever over, you should watch that tongue o' yours. You've got a comfy billet here and Johnson's a good man. You can stay in here until Blair arrives, for I cannae trust you not to do something stupid like running away.'

He went out and locked the door and pocketed the key.

He found Priscilla and asked her to lead him to the tower stair.

He peered up at the empty light-bulb socket. It was above where he stood on a half-landing and could easily be reached by someone of normal height.

'I'll need to search for that light bulb,' he said. 'If, say, a light bulb goes dead in one of the guest's rooms, do they ask you for a replacement?'

'Not usually,' said Priscilla. 'There are spare light bulbs in all the rooms in the shelf under the bedside table.'

'Show me, but not Deborah's room. That'd better be left alone till the forensic team arrives.'

154

Priscilla led the way along the narrow corridor below the tower room. 'Here's an unoccupied guest-room,' she said, opening the door. 'In fact, Hamish, there are going to be a lot of unoccupied guest-rooms next week. Cancellations have been coming in. This has hit us hard. Oh, why didn't you answer the door when I called? If I'd told you what Deborah was up to, you might have thought it worthwhile coming back to the castle with me to warn her.'

'You might haff warned her yourself,' said Hamish stiffly. He went into the room. Three sixty-watt light bulbs lay in their packets on the ledge under the top of the bedside table.

'Three in each room?' he asked.

'No, sometimes two, sometimes one, sometimes four. It varies.'

'Wait a minute, if someone wanted to hide the light bulb taken out of the tower stair, they couldn't just leave it lying alongside the packets.'

'Sorry to disappoint you, but they could. Often there are empty packets, or packets with used light bulbs in them. Some guests put in a new light bulb and put the old one in the packet and then replace it with the others. Or they simply throw the old light bulb into the waste-paper basket. But a used light bulb would not be a sign of guilt.'

'Damn. Damn this whole case. There's something wrong, something nagging at the back of my mind, something someone said.'

He went back to the lounge and began to question the guests again, where they had been at the time Deborah was attacked. They all said they had been in their bedrooms but had no witnesses and, apart from Sean, no one had an alibi.

The contingent from Strathbane arrived headed by Superintendent Peter Daviot, who looked tired and cross. Jimmy Anderson took Hamish aside and explained that Mary French had called for a lawyer immediately she had arrived in Strathbane. Mr Daviot had sat in on the questioning and it had soon transpired that Blair had not a shred of evidence against her. Her lawyer pointed out that a 'mercy killing' in the past was no proof that she had had anything to do with the murder of Peta Gore, who, until this visit north, had been a complete stranger to her. And Mary French was out for blood, threatening to sue for damages. 'She'll be back in today,' said Jimmy ruefully. 'I wish she *had* done it, for she's a nasty piece o' work.'

Hamish was called into the library by Mr Daviot. He gave the superintendent a brief summary of what had happened. 'I also had to interview Matthew Cowper as to his movements on the night of the murder,' added Hamish, not without a tinge of malice. 'He appears to have been overlooked in all the excitement.'

Blair gave Hamish a lowering look but

remained silent.

'While the forensic team search all their rooms again,' said Mr Daviot, 'we had best have them in again, one after another. One of them's a killer, and we are going to stay here until we find out.'

The members of Checkmate and Crystal found Mr Daviot's questioning worse than Blair's. Blair was so rude and angry, one could always react and hit back. But Mr Daviot went on and on persistently, question after question, seemingly tireless. The cool Crystal broke down and confessed that she had been worried Auntie meant to change her will, that her parents had said that when she returned from the north, she was to train for a job, and that she didn't want to work. Jenny told him all about the forestry worker. Everyone told Mr Daviot an awful lot more than, they felt, they had ever told anyone about themselves in their lives before, while the tape recorder hummed and a policewoman from Strathbane sat in a corner and took shorthand notes, Mr Daviot not trusting what he called 'these new-fangled machines.'

By breakfast time none of them had been to bed. Despite the fact that one of them was possibly a killer, they huddled together against the forces of law and order.

Priscilla prepared the breakfast for them all, as the police had just begun a lengthy questioning of Sean. She felt exhausted and

157

wondered why she had gone to all the trouble to feed them when they only picked miserably at their food. Then her mother phoned, alarmed to learn the latest developments, and said she would be home immediately, but the receiver was snatched out of her hand by Colonel Halburton-Smythe. Priscilla repeated her story. Her father said again it was due to her folly that Checkmate had been allowed to come in the first place. He was not going to come back to be badgered by the press as he had been before when there had been that unfortunate shooting, which he was still convinced had been an accident, despite the fact that Hamish Macbeth had proved it to be murder and the murderer had confessed to the killing. Priscilla would just need to cope. There was no question of her mother's returning. It was selfish of Priscilla to be so unfeeling.

Priscilla wearily put down the phone and went in search of Mr Johnson. 'My father's still not coming back,' she said, 'not until this is all over. We'll have to house this lot until the police give up their questioning. I suppose the next thing is that the servants will be giving notice.'

'Not them,' said Mr Johnson cynically. 'This is meat and drink tae them. I've even had women phoning up from the village tae ask if I need any extra help. They've never had such a good gossip in years. We'll need tae work shifts. You go tae bed first and I'll call you in

158

five hours' time and then get a bit o' sleep myself. Would ye look at that!' He pointed out of the window. Bus-loads of uniformed police were arriving.

They both walked to the window and looked out. Not only were there uniformed police but a team of frogmen.

'We're not looking for another body, are we?' he asked.

'Peta's luggage and typewriter,' said Priscilla. 'When I was in for questioning, Mr Daviot was furious that a thorough search had not been made for it. The frogmen will be here to search the lochs and tarns and rivers.'

'Aye, well, off you go and get some sleep.'

Priscilla went up to her room, but she lay awake for a long time, her mind racing. At first the whole hotel venture had been exciting, and the idea of repairing the family fortunes exhilarating. But now she wished she had her home back again, that the lounge could once more be the drawing-room and the bar the morning-room, and all the signs taken down. And they could do it. For the colonel had invested well and wisely this time, thanks to a good broker in the City. But she knew her father would make this set-back an excuse to keep the hotel going. Saved from the hard work by Mr Johnson and herself, he was left free to take all the credit, which he did. It was sad to discover that one's father was a silly, selfish man. The wind of Sutherland was

159

moaning outside, great clouds scudding quickly across a vast sky. The odd and unusual summer was over. It was a time for settling down, for comfortable fishing parties, and shooting parties. She had not even Hamish to turn to, Hamish who *would* go around collecting drips of little girls like Jenny, Jenny with her so-called sensitive feelings about madness. Priscilla's weary mind called up the faces of the suspects. The only one who seemed at all odd was Mary French, with her mixture of arrogance and stupidity, a woman who had killed before. Perhaps Blair had been right all along, thought Priscilla just before she fell asleep.

*   *   *

By evening, Mary French was back, and as the party had been united in their resentment against Peta, now they were united against Mary French and her long, vindictive tales of how she would sue the police and how she had phoned her third cousin, the Earl of Derwent, mark you, and he had been horrified at this evidence of police brutality. Matthew Cowper wondered why on earth he had thought even for a minute that she would make a suitable partner. He felt he would like to strangle her.

And the questioning went on. Mr Daviot would go off for a rest and the questioning would be taken over by Blair. Even John

Taylor, who had been haughty and outraged at the beginning that they should dare to suspect him, had become quiet and subdued. Maria's cheerful face had grown lines of worry and she had become fidgety and irritable. Crystal wandered around in a dressing-gown, not even having bothered to do her hair or face, and was sitting moodily drinking a great deal of champagne. Peter Trumpington and Jessica Fitt sat very close together, but not saying anything. Jenny felt so alone and frightened. She longed for an opportunity to speak to Hamish but he did not emerge from the library.

And then, to her surprise, Matthew Cowper came up to her and said, 'Let's get out of here.'

'We're not allowed to leave,' said Jenny wearily.

'I thought instead of having dinner here, we could go down to that Italian place in the village,' said Matthew. 'We can tell that super where we are.'

'Oh, all right,' said Jenny wearily, 'only don't murder me on the road.'

Matthew gave a surprised laugh but went to the library.

He returned a few moments later. 'We're fixed,' he said. 'They say we can go. We can take my car.'

They went out in silence, conscious of the watching eyes of the policemen, who had returned from a futile search of the moors and were now standing beside their buses, joking

161

and laughing.

'What are they so cheerful about?' asked Jenny as she got into the passenger seat of Matthew's car.

'Overtime,' he said briefly.

He accelerated past the press, who were huddled outside the castle gates, and drove down to Lochdubh. How it had changed from an idyllic village, thought Jenny.

Great waves were surging down the loch, which was lit with fitful gleams of sunlight. Boats bobbed crazily at anchor. Rose-petals from the cottage gardens were blowing down the waterfront and the wind held a chill edge.

The restaurant was full of locals. 'I am looking forward to some Italian cooking,' said Matthew.

It was a small restaurant, formally a craft-shop, with checkered table-cloths and candles in winebottles. It was quite full, but they found a table in a corner. The prices were very cheap, which meant that the locals had begun to patronize it. The restaurant was a mixture of British and Italian cooking.

Jenny and Matthew settled for spaghetti Bolognese and a bottle of Chianti.

'Do you think we'll ever get home to London?' asked Jenny drearily. 'I'll need to phone the office and tell them I've got to be here for a few more days at least.'

'I've already phoned mine,' said Matthew. 'They're all right about it but I am going to

162

have to put up with some pretty tiresome jokes about signing up with a marital agency.'

'Me, too,' said Jenny. 'Why did you join? Can't you get a girl on your own?'

'Don't be rude,' said Matthew huffily. 'I'm a pretty common sort of chap but I want to go far and I need a wife with a good social background. What about you?'

'I'm too shy. I got tired of dating and hoping for Mr Right to come along. It seemed an exciting idea. Also I knew I would be meeting men who were in the same boat. I never thought I would land up in the middle of a murder investigation.'

She looked at Matthew. His normally unexceptional face looked sinister in the flickering candle-light and she added suddenly, 'Did you really steal that whisky?'

'Of course not,' said Matthew hotly, and then, in the same moment, he was overcome with a desire to tell the truth. 'Well, I did,' he said in the next breath. 'I've never stolen anything in my life before and I could easily have afforded to pay for it. I went down to the bar late and they had forgotten to lock it up. I was going to ring the bell and get someone to fetch me something and then I found myself looking at all those bottles, just lying there. It was like turning a kid loose in a sweet-shop. I had pretty poor beginnings and I remember when my mother died, longing for a stiff drink to kill the pain and not being able to afford one. I got an excited feeling, just from pinching it, and then I had the safe knowledge that if I were caught out, I could make some excuse and pay for it. The maids must have seen the bottle in my room, for I never even bothered to hide it. Have you ever stolen anything?'

'No,' said Jenny, and then coloured. 'Just the once. I was going out on this date and one of the other secretaries had this marvellous new shade of lipstick. I noticed she had left it on her desk. So I took it. I was to meet my date in a pub in Chancery Lane, so there I was all lipsticked up and do you know, he stood me up. And the next day, the other secretary raised a song and dance about that missing lipstick. I could have said, "Oh, sorry, here it is. I was going on a date and I borrowed it." But the words stuck in my throat. And she did go on to the senior partner, on and on, and I began to be terrified she'd call the police. I could almost see that lipstick through the leather of my handbag. At lunch-time, I threw the wretched thing into a rubbish bin in the street.'

Matthew raised his glass and grinned. 'Partners in crime,' he said.

Jenny did not return the toast. She looked at him seriously. 'Who did it?' she asked.

He shrugged. 'I don't know. But I think the police are making a mistake focusing solely on us. Why should it be one of us? Look at it this way. Peta was in a sulk and probably wanted to

164

leave. So she decided to borrow the hotel car and drive to London through the night. But she couldn't resist eating and so she took a hamper of goodies with her for the journey. But being a glutton, the quarry was as far as she got. She was sitting there, stuffing her face, when some local madman came on her.'

'If only that could turn out to be the case,' said Jenny wistfully.

'Oh, forget the murder. Tell me about yourself.'

Jenny told him about her idea of taking her law exams, and to her surprise and delight, he was enthusiastic. 'Of course you should,' he said warmly. 'You're a bright girl. You could go far.'

And as Jenny talked on, he eyed her speculatively. If she got over that shyness and diffidence of hers, she would probably be successful. She looked bright enough. And there was bound to be money in the background. As a pair, they could grow together, go far.

The spaghetti arrived, enormous portions of it, and soothed with carbohydrate and alcohol, they talked on until they found they were the last in the restaurant.

'Time to go,' said Matthew reluctantly.

He drove her back to the castle. He thought it might be a start if he kissed her. Perhaps just before they went into the castle. Then they might have a cosy drink in the bar.

165

Then ... who knows?

But as they approached the castle, Superintendent Peter Daviot came out to meet them, his face stern in the half-light. Behind him stood Blair, Hamish, Anderson and Macnab.

'Matthew Cowper,' said the super, 'will you come with us to the library? We have some further questions to ask you.'

'No,' said Jenny desperately. 'You must have made a mistake.'

Mr Daviot ignored her. 'Mr Cowper?'

Head down, Matthew allowed himself to be ushered into the library. 'Sit doon!' barked Blair menacingly.

Matthew sat down in a hard-backed chair facing the long desk behind which the detectives and Hamish were ranged. He felt like the little Cavalier boy in that well-known painting, *When Did You Last See Your Father?*

'Now,' said Mr Daviot, studying a sheaf of notes, 'during an extensive interview, you said you did not know Peta Gore, had never known her or heard anything about her.'

'Yes,' croaked Matthew, his small eyes ranging wildly from face to face.

'The brokerage firm for which you work is Waring's, one of the biggest in the City, is it not?'

'Yes.'

Mr Daviot leaned back in his chair.

'Would it surprise you to know that Peta
166

Gore was one of your firm's biggest clients?'

Matthew looked at the floor.

'And that she once paid a rare visit to the office and was seen talking to you? Shall we start at the beginning again, Mr Cowper? And try to be truthful this time.'

CHAPTER EIGHT

When constabulary duty's to be done,
The policeman's lot is not a happy one!
—W. S. GILBERT

'Oh, *that* Mrs Gore,' said Matthew feebly.

'My theory is this,' said Mr Daviot. 'You were handling shares for Peta Gore and you embezzled her money and you killed her to silence her.'

Hamish noticed that a look of relief flashed across Matthew's eyes. 'No, that's not the case,' he said. He dabbed at his mouth with his handkerchief and then leaned back in his chair, as if forcing all his tensed muscles to relax.

'Waring's is too good a firm for anything like that to happen. There are checks and double-checks. Besides, it's a huge company. I have nothing to do with Mrs Gore's money.'

'But one of the office juniors distinctly remembers her visiting the office and you talking to her.'

That would be Mandy, thought Matthew bitterly. Always gossiping about something.

'Look, I'll come clean with you,' he said. 'I didn't know the Peta Gore here was anything to do with a visiting client I met several years ago. She wasn't as gross then. Had she been, I would have remembered her right away.'

168

'And when did you remember?'

'It was right after she was killed. It all came back into my mind. But she never had had anything to do with me, so I thought, well, why bring it up?' demanded Matthew with a feeble perkiness. 'Can I go now?'

He rose from his chair.

'Sit down,' said Mr Daviot quietly. 'We haven't even started yet.'

Three hours later, Matthew crawled from the room. It had been like some dreadful confessional. They had dragged every bit of his life out of him. How quiet the castle was! The wind had died. He reached his room and stood gloomily in the doorway, surveying the mess. Grey fingerprint dust lay everywhere. His ransacked drawers were open. They were supposed to put everything back the way they found it, or that's what usually happened in the films. The fact that they hadn't made him feel like a criminal. He undressed quickly, switched out the light, and stood at the window for a moment. Moonlight bathed the castle gardens. Beyond the gardens were the moors and above them the mountains. It was all so weird, so strange, like being somewhere far from civilization. His shabby Teddy bear, which went everywhere with him, had been propped neatly on the pillow. He could only be relieved that they hadn't taken it apart.

He climbed into bed and clutched the Teddy to him, praying to the God in whom he never

169

really had believed to get him safely out of Sutherland.

*   *   *

Hamish Macbeth was awake as well, dragged out of sleep by the insistent ringing of the phone in the police station. He crawled to the receiver and picked it up.

'Hullo, copper!' came the breezy voice of his cousin, Rory Grant.

Hamish groaned. 'Don't you ever sleep?'

'I'm on the dog-shift. Nothing's happening. Nothing like what's going on in your neck of the woods. Madmen running around a castle with meat cleavers. Why I'm calling is that I've had our City chap dig around a bit. Do you know this Peta owned a big block of shares in Rag Trade Limited, and Rag Trade Limited is one of Sir Bernard's companies, a company it was once hinted was a front for arms dealing? Now if this Peta had decided to pull out, she might have ruined him. His shares would certainly have slumped.'

'I'm sick and tired o' suspects,' said Hamish waspishly. 'All I want iss one murderer.'

'You're ungrateful. Solve the bloody case yourself then.'

'I'm sorry,' said Hamish wearily. 'How's your friend, the one who went to the funny farm?'

'Back at another funny farm. They let him

170

out. Psychiatrist said there was nothing up with him apart from stress. Then today, he mooned at the editor.'

'You mean he looked silly?'

'No, you old-fashioned thing. He dropped his trousers and waved his bare bum at the editor. Editor phones funny farm in a rage and psychiatrist says editor must have provoked him. So another nut-house is quickly found and guess who had to take him there? Me!'

'You're a tolerant lot,' marvelled Hamish. 'I would haff thought he would just haff been fired.'

'Well, he's been with the paper for yonks, and a very respected soul. Just went round the twist sudden-like, although I suppose there have been pointers for a time. He came in with a tonsure last year.'

'Surely that told ye something?'

'No. Men and women get a reputation of being great eccentrics and in the meantime no one really notices they're stark-raving bonkers.'

'What job does this friend of yours do on the paper?'

'Religious correspondent.'

'Oh, dear. Well, if you can dig up any madness that applies to any of them up here, let me know.'

'Expect more guests, that I do know,' said Rory.

'Who?'

171

'Crystal Debenham's parents are rushing up to collect their chick, or that's what they said when interviewed today. Jenny Trask's mother is also heading north, and Mr and Mrs Freemantle, Deborah's parents.'

'I could do without them,' said Hamish. 'I'll see if I can get them billeted elsewhere. I've got enough people on my hands and I don't want my suspects diluted.'

He said goodbye to Rory and went back to bed. If only he could solve the case before these relatives arrived on the scene.

The faces of them all and what they had said went running through his mind.

He awoke suddenly at six in the morning and stared at the ceiling. It had been there, in his dreams, the clue to it all. There was one piece that did not fit. He was looking for a madman or madwoman, that he now knew. Jenny had been right. One of them was mad, mad enough to hold Peta down and shove an apple in her mouth.

He washed and dressed and went down to the harbour, where the fishing boats were coming in. He needed two men, two men who were prepared to lie. Archie Maclean was too much of a risk. He would gossip about it all beforehand. Then he saw the Nairn brothers, Luke and Paul, walking along the harbour. They were both huge men, over six feet tall, with mild, childlike eyes.

'Could you come back to the police station

172

with me?' said Hamish.

'Whit hae we done?' demanded Paul suspiciously.

'Nothing. I want you both to do me a favour.'

They followed him along to the police station and into the narrow kitchen at the back.

'Now,' said Hamish, 'I want you both tae tell one great whopping lie for me.'

'And whit's in it for us?' asked Luke.

'You will be helping to trap a murderer.'

Luke leaned back in his chair so that he could look through the inner open door of the kitchen which led into the living-room.

'My, thon's the grand TV set ye hae there, Hamish,' he said. 'Paul and me dinnae hae one. We're lodging at Mrs Gunn's ower the back and she willnae let us watch hers. Keeps it in her bedroom.'

'This iss the blackmail,' said Hamish hotly.

'Aye, well,' said Paul as he and his brother rose to their feet, 'we'd best be off.'

'Wait!' said Hamish. 'All right, you can have the TV. Sit down and I'll tell you what you have to do.'

*   *   *

Priscilla could feel her bad temper rising. Another lousy night's sleep and Sean too hungover to help with the breakfast. The maids

173

were there, but they were too over-excited and gossipy and kept dropping things and forgetting things.

Then she had to deal with the guests. 'Are we ever going to get out of here?' demanded John Taylor. He was on edge.

'I'm afraid that is up to the police,' said Priscilla. 'But unless an arrest is made today, I think they will probably go on questioning you all.'

'It's all snobbery,' said Mary French crossly, but her twitching face showing her nervousness. 'I don't believe they have bothered to question any of the staff. That man Blair has a chip on his shoulder. He wants to get at us because we are his social superiors.'

'So much for John Major's classless society,' said Matthew. 'Can't see that ever happening with people like you around, Mary.'

'Oh,' retorted Mary nastily, her eyes narrowing, acumen replacing vanity in her distress, 'you were only sucking up to me because you wanted a foot up the social ladder, or perhaps we shouldn't mention that!'

'What did the police want to see you about, Matthew?' asked Sir Bernard.

'They found out that Peta dealt with the company I work for and that I had once met her,' said Matthew. 'I really didn't remember I'd ever met her until after the murder and then I thought it might look a bit suspicious. God, they're digging into backgrounds all over the

174

City. I'll be lucky if I have a job to go back to.'

Sir Bernard stared at the table-cloth. 'Bastards,' he muttered.

Only Jenny looked at all composed. She knew her mother would be there that day. She would see the police and take her home. Her mother had said on the phone that she had contacted the law offices where Jenny worked and they had agreed that Jenny could have a few days at home to recuperate. She glanced at Matthew Cowper. Prince Charming had turned into a frog. She noticed his too-wide mouth and too-small eyes, his showy cravat, and the badge of his blazer, which did not stand for any school, club, or university, only the product of some designer's mind. And yet, last night he had seemed so likeable, a soul mate, and if the police hadn't been waiting on the doorstep, she would have let him kiss her.

Deborah had lost a lot of her bounce. She was glad her parents were coming. It had all been a nightmare. Priscilla was pouring coffee. Deborah summoned her by snapping her fingers. Jenny noticed that Priscilla's mouth tightened a little but she went over to Deborah and said politely, 'Miss Freemantle?'

'There is still no light on the tower stair,' said Deborah. 'See to it.'

Priscilla nodded and moved off. What a terrible job she has, thought Jenny. Imagine having to endure being spoken to like that.

Priscilla found Mr Johnson. 'King George

175

the Second is complaining about no light on the tower stair. I'll go and fix it by taking one of the bulbs out of the bedrooms.'

'George the Second?'

'Deborah Freemantle.'

'Aye, she's got a look o' the House of Hanover. But don't take one out of the bedrooms; I'll give you one from the stock in the office.'

'Why?'

'Saving money. A forty-watt's good enough for the stairs and passages; sixty-watt for the bedrooms.'

'But that means—' Priscilla wrestled with her thoughts—'that we've been looking for a sixty-watt bulb, not a forty-watt.'

'So what? They didn't find anything.'

'Wait a minute. All someone had to do was to take the forty-watt bulb out of the tower stair,' said Priscilla, 'and then take it to their room, unplug one of the sixty-watt and leave it lying harmlessly on the beside table and put in a forty-watt, put the lampshade over it, and there you are!'

'And here's the police,' said Mr Johnson.

Hamish was coming into the entrance hall with the detectives from Strathbane. Priscilla rushed to him and explained about the light bulbs.

The superintendent was listening as well. He ordered a policeman to inform the guests that they were not to go up to their rooms until they

176

were told they could do so.

'I think I know whose bedroom to go to first,' said Hamish. Right up until Priscilla had told him about the light bulb, he had been planning to send Paul and Luke, who would arrive in a few moments, home. If he was wrong, then Paul and Luke would be in bad trouble and he would need to get them out of it by telling Daviot he had bribed them to lie. 'I'm pretty sure who the murderer is.'

'Tell us,' sneered Blair.

'That bedroom first,' said Hamish.

'I'll go up with Hamish,' said Mr Daviot. 'You stay down here, Blair, and make sure none of them escapes.'

Blair cast a look of loathing at Hamish.

Hamish led the way into of one of the Checkmate party's bedrooms and looked around. There was one overhead light with a sixty-watt bulb in it. But there were two bulbs, one on either side of the bed. He lifted the shade of the first and felt a sour taste of failure in his mouth. Sixty-watt. He went slowly to the other while Mr Daviot watched him impatiently. Hamish felt like a man with one last chance at the Sixty-Four Thousand Dollar Question. He raised the lampshade and drew a long breath. 'It's a forty-watt bulb,' he said.

'We can't arrest someone on such flimsy evidence,' protested the superintendent. 'We need more proof.'

'I hae the proof,' said Hamish. 'Two

177

witnesses.'

'Two witnesses! Why didn't they come forward before?'

'They're fishermen. They say they haven't been reading the newspapers and don't have a television set, but it's my belief they were poaching. If you want your murderer, you'll have to turn a blind eye to that.'

'But fishermen go out at night!'

'Well, they werenae out fishing that night,' said Hamish crossly. 'Don't you want the murderer? Look, let me confront this person. If I'm wrong, I'll take the rap.'

'Oh, very well, Macbeth.' No Hamish now. 'And do remember to address me as "sir" in future.'

Blair, Anderson, Macnab and two police officers were ushered into the library. 'Who is it?' Blair kept demanding crossly.

Mr Daviot took his place behind the desk and said, 'Send in Mr John Taylor.'

'Whit?' roared Blair. 'A Queen's Counsel commit a murder? Yer away wi' the fairies this time, Macbeth. I hivnae heard sich a—'

'*If* you don't mind,' said the superintendent icily.

John Taylor came in and sat down without fuss. He looked totally composed. He was dressed in a pin-striped suit and impeccable shirt and silk tie, just as if he were ready to go to the Old Bailey.

'I will let you begin the questioning,

178

Macbeth,' said Mr Daviot heavily and Blair grinned. Daviot obviously knew Hamish was making a fool of himself.

'Mr Taylor,' said Hamish, the sibilancy of his accent strongly marked as it always was when he was nervous or excited, 'I haff the good reason to believe that you murdered Mrs Peta Gore by stuffing an apple in her mouth and pinching her nostrils so that she died of suffocation. I also believe that you tried to murder Deborah Freemantle. In the latter case, you removed the bulb from the tower stair and put in one of the lamps in your room, substituting it for the sixty-watt bulb that was already there.'

'I did no such thing,' said the lawyer calmly.

'Furthermore,' Hamish went on, 'I haff the two witnesses, Paul and Luke Nairn, who saw you up at the quarry with Peta Gore on the night of her death, having a moonlight picnic.'

The only sign of emotion about John Taylor was his long thin hands, which he clasped around one pointed knee. 'Witnesses?' he said cynically. 'They took a long time to come forward.'

'I'll bring them in.' Hamish nodded to the policeman on guard at the door, who opened it and shouted, 'Paul and Luke Nairn.'

Just like a courtroom, thought John.

The large brothers shuffled in and stood sheepishly in the middle of the room, still in their oilskins and smelling strongly of fish.

179

'We'll start with you, Luke,' said Hamish.
'Chust tell us in your own words what you
saw.' Meaning I hope you remember my
words, thought Hamish desperately.

'We wass up by the quarry when we heard
talking,' said Luke. 'It wass the bright moonlit
night. We saw this man here as clear as day. He
was pouring wine. He wass sitting on the
ground. Beside him wass a great fat wumman
and she was shoving a meat-pie in her mouth. I
haff never seen the like. I haff never seen
anyone eat a meat-pie like that, not even
Geordie over at Crask. We didnae stop, Paul
and me, we walked on a bittie, and we wass
admiring the view when behind us, from the
direction o' the quarry, we heard a scrabbling,
choking sort o' sound and Paul here, he says,
Nae wunner she's choking, the way she eats.'

He fell silent. A clock ticked in the corner of
the room. John Taylor sat very still. Witnesses?
thought Blair, privately delighted. A couple of
liars. Admire the view! Havers.

And then John opened his mouth and spoke.
'I did it, yes,' he said.

Hamish charged him while the
superintendent leaned back in his chair, limp
with relief.

Hamish dismissed Paul and Luke. Then he
asked John, 'What happened? Take it slowly.
No one heard a car driving off that night.
Why?'

'Chance,' said John wearily. 'I thought
180

afterwards I was a master criminal, but I simply got away with things by being a complete amateur. I wanted to get even with my son and daughter for having been cruel to me. They were expecting to inherit my money. It was not enough revenge to simply leave it to some charity. I wanted them to suffer. I planned to marry and bear children, but when I got here, I realized the folly of it all. Who was going to look at an old man like me?

'Then came Peta's news of her millions. That one would have been happy to marry anyone to spite Maria. I thought, I'll marry her and then I'll be fabulously rich and *then* I shall tell my ungrateful son and daughter that they aren't getting anything. I went to her room and suggested we slip off for a romantic picnic at midnight. The awful creature was thrilled at the idea. I went down to the kitchen and packed up one of those picnic hampers with what I could find. I knew the hotel cars often had the keys left in them. I took the Volvo. Peta came out.

'The car would not start. And would you believe it, the very sight of her gross figure in the moonlight had made me change my mind. I said, 'Let's leave it.' No, she had to try one of the other cars but the keys were missing from those. I suppose they take them in for the night but because Jenny had used the Volvo, the keys had been left in it.

'So I decided that was that and was relieved.

181

But she then suggested I get in the Volvo and she would push it down the drive, which was on a slope. I tried to persuade her to abandon the project but she insisted. She pushed the car down the drive and the engine started.'

'Was the quarry your idea?' asked Hamish.

'No, hers. She couldn't wait to eat, you see. I decided to make the best of a bad job. She guzzled and slobbered. I drank the wine. To pass the time I told her about the hurt that had been inflicted on me by my children saying I was boring. She finished the meat-pie and wiped her mouth and said with a coarse laugh, "Well, you are a bit of an old stick, aren't you? If I was one of your kids, I'd run a mile."

'One minute I was sitting there and the next minute I had pushed her on her back and rammed the apple into her mouth. I remember shouting something, but I don't know what. I grabbed her nose with my fingers and squeezed it. I had that done to me at school and I remembered it hurt very much. That's all I really wanted to do. Hurt her. But she was suddenly still and I realized I had killed her.

'I was terrified. I gathered up all the stuff in the hamper, every scrap, every crumb I could see and wandered across the moors until I came to a peatbog. I weighed it down with a boulder and sank it. I returned to the car and drove to the castle.

'Oh, I thought I was so clever. I wore gloves. I typed the note on her machine and then

182

packed her clothes and carried the lot out again. I had left the car at the castle gates. I got rid of her luggage and her typewriter in the same peatbog. If I had been really clever, I would have put her body in the peatbog as well, but I could not bear to touch her.

'Once it was all over, I felt rested, strangely peaceful, as if someone else had done the murder. I thought the fates were protecting me because I had completely forgotten about fingerprints in the car, for I had not worn gloves the time I drove off with her.

'When Jenny left the car with the windows open and then I saw the maids cleaning it out, I remembered the fingerprints and was delighted that a benign Providence was taking care of me. My shoulders were aching, for I had pushed the car back up the slope the last bit to the front of the castle in case the noise of the engine would wake anyone, but apart from that I felt light-headed and well.'

'So what about Deborah?' asked Hamish gently.

'When she said, "I saw you do it," I thought at first, and rightly, as it turned out, that she was showing off, that she knew nothing. But you see, I had quite forgotten in my mind until then that I had killed Peta. It all came back, the horror of it. I could see the faces of all those I had prosecuted in the past rising to haunt me. I was consumed with such a rage against her. Again, it was the luck of the amateur. I suppose

183

anyone could have seen me going into the kitchen. I was amazed it was not locked up. I did not go to get the meat cleaver. Somehow, I was returning to the scene of my earlier crime, or rather, the beginning of it. I switched on the light and there on the chopping block lay that meat cleaver. I picked it up. It felt good in my hand. I have a dim memory of going up the tower stairs and taking the light bulb out and slipping it in my pocket. Then nothing until that terrible screaming. I ran to my room and quickly took a bulb out of the bedside light and put the bulb from the tower stair in the socket instead.' He let out a ragged sigh. 'I'm glad it's all over.'

Mr Daviot said to the policeman at the door, 'Take Mr Taylor out to the car. Macnab and Anderson, go with him. I will follow in the other car with Blair.'

When they had gone, Mr Daviot turned to Hamish. 'Well done,' he said. 'How did you arrive at such a conclusion ... or did you have any help?' He looked at Blair, who looked pleadingly at Hamish and mouthed, 'Central heating.' For Blair had promised Hamish at the end of the last case that in return for Hamish's allowing him the credit, he would see to it that central heating was installed in the Lochdubh police station.

But Hamish was weary of Blair, weary of his spite and stupidity and malice. 'No, I worked it out myself,' he said, avoiding Blair's look of

184

venom. Blair got to his feet. 'Ah'll jist catch up wi' the others,' he said.

'Oh, very well.' Mr Daviot looked surprised. Blair usually stuck to him like a shadow, which was why Blair was forgiven such a lot. Mr Daviot would never admit he liked crawlers, but Blair was so very good at it, always remembering to send flowers on Mrs Daviot's birthday, always saying loudly that Mr Peter Daviot was the best superintendent in the country.

'Now, Hamish,' said Mr Daviot when Blair had gone.

'It was such a long shot,' said Hamish. 'I knew, I think I had known all along, that I was looking for someone mad, or at least temporarily insane. And then it came to me, something my cousin said about eccentrics and then about John Taylor being a great old character. John Taylor had once punched a policeman in the face outside the Old Bailey for not showing him due respect. That was all. Then I thought, there's madness. An eminent Q.C. does not lose his rag like that, particularly when that Q.C. was in the wrong. An eminent Q.C. does not sign up with a marital agency, nor does he plan to marry and start a family at his age. It does not happen. Something was badly wrong with John Taylor. No one else fitted the picture. I became convinced that this was no carefully planned murder but simply committed by someone who had lost his mind.

I may as well tell you now that it is no use producing the Nairn brothers in court. They lied. I put them up to it.'

Peter Daviot looked at him appalled. 'It is just as well we have his taped statement, and in front of so many witnesses. Man, man, what a scandal if you had been wrong.'

'Aye, well, by the time I got to the castle, I thought I wass the madman,' said Hamish, himself appalled at the enormity of what he had done. 'I wass going to send the Nairn brothers home after you started the questioning again and then Priscilla told me about the light bulbs, and as you know, we found the missing light bulb in John Taylor's room. When Mr Taylor told me that he had wanted to marry again because he was lonely, he began to cry and I remember thinking at the time that he wass a man on the verge of a nervous breakdown, but for a while I thought it might be the strain of him finding himself in the middle of a murder inquiry.'

'I should give you a row for the gamble you took,' said Mr Daviot severely, 'but on the other hand, I am relieved this dreadful case is over. This will mean promotion for you, Hamish.'

Hamish looked startled. 'I am not looking for the promotion,' he said desperately. 'But if you could see you way to getting some central heating put in the police station...'

'Always the modest lad, Hamish. Oh, I've

heard rumours flying about that it was you who solved those last murders and let Blair take the credit. Blair's a good, solid policeman, but he does not have your flair. How many bedrooms do you have in that police station?'

Hamish eyed him warily. 'Mine and a small spare one I use if any of my little brothers and sisters are visiting.'

'Excellent. I think you should be promoted to sergeant and we'll send some young lad up to help you. I have the very policeman in mind.'

Hamish pleaded and protested, but Mr Daviot was adamant. 'You should be thinking of your future, Hamish. You'll be getting married to your Priscilla soon, or so my wife believes, and you'll need the extra pay. It's time I took your career in hand.'

Hamish was still protesting when he followed Mr Daviot out to his car. Blair was sitting moodily behind the wheel.

'You had better go home and type up your statement,' said Mr Daviot. 'Give my regards to Priscilla and tell her my wife was asking for her.'

Mr Daviot got in and Blair shot off with an angry grinding of gears.

Hamish went wearily to his Land Rover and drove to the police station. As he got out, two large figures loomed up. The Nairn brothers.

'If it iss all right wi' you,' said Luke cheerfully, 'we'll hae that telly now.'

CHAPTER NINE

Life is just one damned thing after another.
                    —FRANK O'MALLEY (attributed)

John Taylor stood patiently after turning out his pockets. He had surrendered his braces, tie and shoe-laces. 'I'd better have those pills,' he said, pointing to a pharmacist's bottle which lay among the other items taken from him.

The custody sergeant picked it up. 'What is it?' The label was worn.

'My heart medicine,' said John gently. 'I am sure you would not want me to die in one of your cells.'

The custody sergeant shook out a couple of white pills from the bottle. 'I'll jist keep these and hae them examined.'

John was led to a cell in Strathbane police headquarters. He knew he would be transferred to prison in the morning. 'You won't have eaten, sir,' said the young policeman who had escorted him to his cell. 'Can I get ye some mutton-pie and chips frae the canteen?'

John shuddered fastidiously. 'I am not hungry. But I would like a couple of bottles of mineral water, if you would be so kind.' He gave a flickering smile. 'I am very thirsty.'

The mineral water was delivered along with

a tray of food and he was urged to eat. The day wore on, light faded outside his cell, and the sea-gulls of Strathbane screamed like lost souls as they scavenged the streets.

By late evening, John had still not eaten anything but he asked for pen and paper.

He wrote a letter to his son and daughter. In it, he said he was sure they would enjoy his money. He was only delighted they would have to suffer the publicity that their father was a murderer. All his brief love for them he had felt when he had been talking to Hamish had gone. He hated them both. He quoted from *King Lear*. He reminded them it was sharper than a serpent's tooth to have a thankless child. He folded the paper neatly and put it squarely in the middle of the small table in his cell.

Then he opened the first of the bottles of mineral water and doggedly began to swallow all the small pills in the pharmacist's bottle.

The analysis of the pills came through in the morning. They were extremely strong barbiturates. Cursing and sweating, the duty sergeant ran to John Taylor's cell.

He was lying peacefully. There was only a faint flicker of life in his pulse. They rushed him to hospital, but he was dead on arrival.

* * *

Hamish Macbeth heard the news of John's death later in the day. He thought sourly that all the inquiries that would be buzzing about Strathbane, first the wrongful arrest of Mary French, and now this, would keep everyone too busy to think about his promotion or landing some young constable in his home.

He decided to go up to the castle and see how Priscilla was.

Priscilla was dealing with the home-coming of her parents. They had arrived bringing their Caithness hosts, Mr and Mrs Turnbull, with them, along with Jamie Turnbull, their son, who was home on leave from his regiment. It was typical of her father not to phone to find out if there were any spare rooms, thought Priscilla furiously. Actually there were, for all had left, with the exception of Jenny Trask and her mother, a small capable woman who said they would have a few days' rest after 'little' Jenny's ordeal before travelling south. But the phone had been ringing steadily with bookings as the news of the arrest and subsequent death of the murderer got out. A murderer at large was bad for business. A murder solved gave the hotel an interesting cachet, particularly as the murderer had not turned out to be one of those dreadful common people.

'I am glad to see you, Mr and Mrs Turnbull and Jamie,' said Priscilla firmly, 'but you can only stay a few days. Our books are getting full again.'

'What is this?' demanded the colonel, bristling. 'May I remind you, dear girl, that this is *my* hotel, a hotel which I started and made prosper?'

Hamish strolled in to hear that last sentence. Priscilla stood facing her father, cool and calm as usual, and then suddenly she cracked. 'You've done bloody nothing to get this hotel off the ground. Nothing! I've worked and slaved, and so has Mother, while you strut around annoying the guests and then we have to soothe them down. You didn't even bother to come back to help me when you knew there had been a murder committed. The attack on Deborah didn't even move you. Oh, no! I've got to stay here and cope with the lot, me and Mr Johnson. I'm tired of your poncing, your vanity, and your bullying. Get stuffed, Daddy dear!'

She stormed off. The colonel stood, his mouth opening and shutting. 'Why don't we all go into the bar?' said Mrs Halburton-Smythe brightly. 'I'm sure we could all do with a drink.' And propelling her husband in front of her and Mr and Mrs Turnbull, she shooed them toward the bar like a fussy mother hen shepherding her chicks.

Jamie Turnbull found Priscilla in the kitchen. 'You've had a hard time,' he said. He was a tall, pleasant-looking young man. 'Believe me, I tried to get your father to go home, but he wouldn't budge.'

'It's all right now,' said Priscilla weakly. 'I wish I hadn't lost my temper.'

191

'He needed a telling off. Look, you're frazzled to bits. Why don't you come with me and we'll go off for a drive, have dinner somewhere and keep away from this work-house.'

'Oh, I'd love that,' said Priscilla. 'Once Daddy's recovered from the shock, he'll be raging about the place all day.'

The kitchen door opened and Hamish Macbeth looked in. 'All right, Priscilla?' he asked. 'I wass wondering if you felt like a bite to eat at that new Italian place this evening?' Suddenly Priscilla remembered looking down from the castle and seeing Jenny kissing him. 'I already have a dinner date, Hamish,' she said coldly. 'But if you're at a loose end, your little friend Jenny's still about.' Hamish retreated and banged the kitchen door. He walked moodily out to the Land Rover and stood beside it, kicking the gravel in the drive. He had seen Priscilla come to life. She had been magnificent when she had given that old scunner of a father of hers the dressing down he so much deserved. And he had been looking forward to telling her about the case. But all she wanted to do was go off with Jamie Turnbull, Jamie Turnbull who, as Hamish knew, was rich, popular, and a captain in a Highland regiment. Jenny, indeed! He was not interested in Jenny.

And then there was Jenny herself, walking towards him with a grey-haired woman who, he guessed, was probably her mother.

'Hamish,' cried Jenny. 'I was coming to see you. You have been so awfully clever. Do tell Mummy and me how you solved the case.'

'I haven't the time at the moment,' said Hamish.

'Maybe later,' urged Jenny.

'My daughter tells me there's a good Italian restaurant in the village,' said Mrs Trask. 'We would be honoured if you would join us for dinner tonight. I owe you a great debt of thanks. If it had not been for your intelligence and capability, my poor daughter might still be under suspicion of murder.'

'She was never that,' said Hamish, although her words were balm to his soul so recently wounded by Priscilla.

Priscilla came out of the castle with Jamie. They got into Jamie's Jaguar and roared off.

Hamish watched them go with bleak eyes.

'So please say you will come,' urged Mrs Trask.

'Yes, I'd be delighted,' said Hamish firmly.

'Good, we'll meet you there at seven o'clock.'

Hamish drove back to the village. The village spinsters, Jessie and Nessie Currie, were waiting for him outside the police station.

'Just imagine!' cried Jessie. 'A lawyer being involved in drug smuggling! In drug smuggling!'

'And it's just said on the radio that he took

193

his own life,' said Nessie. 'Did he inject himself with crack?'

'No,' said Hamish crossly. 'He was a madman who killed by mistake. Had he lived, the charge would probably have been reduced from murder to culpable homicide.'

'You said it was the drugs,' said Jessie, disappointed. 'Not much of a policeman, are you? Not much of a policeman.'

'Run along, ladies,' said Hamish. 'I have work to do.'

He went into the police station by the kitchen door at the back. His dog, Towser, who had been feeling neglected during the case, stared at him accusingly. He had had no walks, only let out into the field at the back, and, worse than that, Hamish had been feeding him dog food, and Towser liked people food. 'I sometimes think you're the only friend I've got, Towser,' said Hamish. The yellowish mongrel turned his back on him as if to remind him that even that was in doubt.

Hamish looked at the kitchen. The sink was piled high with dirty dishes. He sighed and went back out to the butcher's, where he bought a pound of liver. He returned and cooked it up and then, when it was cool, cut it up and gave it to Towser. Then he washed the dishes while the dog ate and then cleaned the rest of the kitchen. He moved to the remainder of the house, changing the sheets on the bed, washing them by hand because he had not yet got a washing machine and hanging them out in the back garden to dry. He then took Towser for a long walk. A stiff breeze was sending choppy angry little waves splashing on the beach, but it gradually entered his soul that murder had left Lochdubh, that everything was back to normal, and he had a pleasant dinner to look forward to ... and sod Priscilla.

By evening, he felt it had all been some sort of nightmare. The police station was clean, and warm from the fire in the kitchen stove. Towser was happily stretched out before it. He phoned his cousin in London to tell him about the case and then he bathed and dressed in a clean shirt and tie and his one pair of good trousers.

Jenny and her mother were already there and waiting for him when he arrived at the restaurant. As soon as the pre-dinner drinks had been served, he was pressed to tell them all about it.

'It was the madness of it all,' said Hamish. 'That was the clue. Your daughter helped a lot, Mrs Trask.'

'She's a bright girl,' said Mrs Trask fondly and patted her daughter's hand. 'But how did she help?'

'She said she was upset because she sensed one of them was mad. I found myself thinking about that. Then my cousin, Rory, who works for a newspaper, said the religious correspondent had been taken off to a mental asylum. I talked to him again before coming

195

here, and he was saying how odd it was that in newspapers, the church, law, or various other places which house eccentrics, that someone can be going quite mad and yet all that happens for a long time is that they build up the reputation of being a "great old character." Now John Taylor had punched a policeman in the face outside the Old Bailey for trying to stop him parking on a double-yellow line. You would have thought that would have been the end of Mr Taylor's career, but not a bit of it. The policeman did not press charges, but it got in the newspapers and John Taylor received very affectionate comments from various columnists.'

'For attacking a policeman!' exclaimed Mrs Trask.

'My cousin, Rory, said that journalists and readers are fed up with the strict parking laws in London. So Mr Taylor's mad behaviour was treated as that of a great old character who had simply done what a great deal of the public and press feel like doing when accused of a parking offence.' Warming to his subject under their admiring gaze, Hamish went on to tell them about the light bulb.

'So the difficulty in solving the case,' said Mrs Trask shrewdly, 'was because the murder was done by a rank amateur?'

'A lucky one, too,' said Hamish.

The door of the restaurant opened and Priscilla came in with Jamie. They sat at a table by the window that had just been vacated. Priscilla was wearing a short scarlet wool dress with a black patent-leather belt. Jamie had changed into a dark, beautifully tailored suit for dinner. He looked smooth and rugged at the same time, like a man in an aftershave-lotion advertisement.

'It is interesting,' Mrs Trask was saying, 'because the murder was solved in such an amateur way.'

'What?' said Hamish, wrenching his eyes away from Priscilla.

'Mummy!' protested Jenny.

'Well, one could hardly expect you to be an expert,' said Mrs Trask in a kindly voice. 'You're only a village policeman. But it is amusing, when you think of it; an amateur murder which could only probably have been solved by another amateur.'

'Mummy, you'd better explain,' said Jenny in an agonized voice. 'You're being quite rude.'

Jamie was talking away but Priscilla was not listening to him. She was listening instead to Mrs Trask, who had a carrying voice.

'I mean . . .' Mrs Trask rolled linguine neatly round her fork and popped it in her mouth before going on, 'if that girl at the hotel hadn't discovered about the light bulbs, you would have had nothing other to go on but some trumped-up evidence that would have fallen on its face if you ever got the case to court.'

'Who said it was trumped-up evidence?'

197

demanded Hamish stiffly.

'Jenny said two local men were called into the library to give evidence. They were not even taken off to Strathbane to make statements, which they surely should have been if they were witnesses and telling the truth. Jenny met them waiting at reception and one of them told her that they were witnesses to the murder. But it was in the newspapers, on radio and on television, and surely every detail of the case was chewed over in this little village, and yet two locals did not come forward at the time! Do you know what I think?'

'No,' said Hamish crossly.

'I think you got them to say they saw something to startle John Taylor into an admission of guilt.' She shook her head and gave a patronizing laugh. 'So Highland. So amateur.'

'I really cannot be bothered arguing with you,' said Hamish.

'Oh, Mummy, Hamish is the one who persuaded me to sit for my bar exams.'

'I'm not surprised. You are not married, are you, Mr Macbeth?'

'No.'

'Well, I hold old-fashioned views. A young girl like Jenny should be thinking of marriage and not a career. If I had known of this dating agency, I would have stopped it. Jenny's going to come home to live with her parents for a bit.'

'You never said anything about that,'

198

gasped Jenny, thinking of her little flat in South Kensington and her freedom.

'I've made up my mind. There are plenty of suitable men in Haywards Heath, and law offices there, too, if you want to go on earning pocket money.'

'But *Mummy*.'

'Now, all this murder business has quite turned your head. You'll see sense when you get home.'

Jenny grasped the edge of the table firmly with both hands. 'I'm taking my law exams and that's that!'

'I'm not going to support you in this folly, and neither is Daddy.'

'Then I'll get a grant. You can't stop me.'

'Well, now,' said Mrs Trask smoothly, 'I think we should save these family rows for a less public place, Jenny. You should not have put such a silly idea into her head, Mr Macbeth.'

'I don't think it silly,' said Hamish. 'Time she grew up.'

Mrs Trask finished the last of her linguine and then stood up. 'I am leaving. Come along, Jenny.'

'No,' said Jenny stubbornly.

'I shall see you later, young miss, and talk some sense into your head.'

She walked out, without, Hamish noticed gloomily, paying the bill.

Priscilla came up to their table. 'Mind if we

199

join you?'

Hamish looked up at her with relief in his eyes. 'Not at all.'

'So you're the bobby that solved the case,' said Jamie.

'Aye, but I don't want to talk about it.'

Jenny, however, burst into speech, about how *unfair* it all was that her mother would not let her take a law degree. Hamish sat in stony silence, Priscilla looked preoccupied, so good-natured Jamie turned a friendly ear to Jenny's complaints and soon they were talking like old friends.

As coffee was about to be served, Hamish said abruptly, 'I'm tired. I think I'll go home.'

'I'll walk along with you. I want to tell you something,' said Priscilla. 'Be back in a minute, Jamie.'

They went outside and walked in silence along to the police station. 'Coffee here?' suggested Hamish. 'You havenae told me yet what it wass you wanted tae talk to me about.'

'Yes, all right,' said Priscilla, following him in. 'I didn't want to say anything in particular, Hamish. But I did hear what that horrible Trask woman was saying about you being an amateur and thought you might need soothing. Besides, you left Jamie with the bill that Mrs Trask did not pay.'

'So I did,' said Hamish with a slow smile. 'I didn't think of that. Towser, get your paws off Priscilla.'

'Leave the dog alone,' said Priscilla. 'He doesn't bother me.'

Hamish made two mugs of coffee and then sat down.

He told her all about the case and then about his promotion to sergeant and ended with, 'That Trask woman did hurt. She was right, you know. I could have made a terrible mistake. A rank amateur, that's me.'

'You've always relied on your intuition before, Hamish. You're to be congratulated.'

'Well, my intuition's not doing me much good at the moment,' he said, studying her. 'Why were you so mad at me?'

Priscilla opened her mouth to lie, to say it was because she had been wrought up after the row with her father, but she found herself saying, 'I saw Jenny kissing you.'

'Oh, thon. Well, Priscilla, she wass kissing me, I wasnae kissing her.'

'Silly of me. But you really do encourage that sort of weak female.'

He smiled into her eyes. 'I'd rather be kissing a strong one.'

He leaned towards her. Priscilla closed her eyes. The kitchen was warm and cosy with the stove crackling and the smell of coffee.

And then there was a hammering at the door.

'Damn. That's probably Jenny and Jamie,' said Hamish. 'Wait here. I'll get rid of them.'

He opened the door. A policeman stood

201

there, a very clean, neat, precise-looking policeman with light eyes, a thin narrow mouth and a very pointed nose.

He removed his cap, revealing short greased hair.

'Constable Willie Lamont,' he said. 'My stuff's in the car. Will I bring it in, sir?'

'What stuff?' said Hamish in dismay.

'I am moving in, Sergeant Macbeth. I am your new constable.'

'It's all right,' said Priscilla with a rueful laugh. 'I'm going. Can I borrow your car, Hamish? I'll send one of the hotel staff back with it.'

'Not the police car!' said Willie Lamont.

'Yes, the police car,' retorted Hamish crossly.

'Civilians are not allowed to drive police vehicles at any time,' said Willie primly. 'In the rule book, page nine, paragraph five, it says—'

'Take the car, Priscilla,' ordered Hamish.

'Don't worry. Jamie's probably looking for me.'

Priscilla went out into the twilight. Poor Hamish! What an awful copper he'd got saddled with. Probably Blair's choice, she thought, not knowing it was Daviot's.

Mrs Wellington, the minister's wife, drove up and stopped beside Priscilla. 'Can I give you a lift?' she asked.

Priscilla hesitated. Jamie's Jaguar was still parked outside the restaurant, but she did not feel like going back to join him. Besides, he appeared delighted with Jenny.

'Thanks, Mrs Wellington,' she said, climbing into the battered station wagon.

* * *

Inside the restaurant, Jamie and Jenny were down to the end of their second bottle of wine. He was really deliciously handsome, thought Jenny, and they had so much in common.

'What about a brandy for the road?' asked Jamie.

Jenny smiled. 'I'd love that. Do you know, I just realized one marvellous thing, I get money from a family trust and Mummy can't stop that, so I can take my law exams.'

'Forget about the brandy,' said Jamie. 'This calls for champagne!'

Jenny giggled. He was really quite divine. And then a nasty voice in her head reminded her that Brian Mulligan had seemed really divine and then Matthew Cowper. She mentally jumped on that voice. Jamie was really wonderful. So strong, so masterful.

She wondered what it would be like to be a captain's wife.